Cesare Pavese

THE MOON AND THE BONFIRE

Translated from the Italian by
Louise Sinclair

Translated from the Italian *La Luna e i Falò*

Copyright © 1950 Giulio Einaudi Editore S.p.A.

This translation first published by Peter Owen Limited, London, 1952

Quartet Books edition, 1978

Sceptre edition, 1988

Sceptre is an imprint of Hodder and Stoughton Paperbacks, a division of Hodder and Stoughton Limited.

British Library C.I.P.

Pavese, Cesare
  The moon and the bonfire.
  I. Title   II. La luna e i falô.
  English
  853'.912[F]   PQ4835.A846

  ISBN 0-340-42433-8

Printed and bound in Great Britain for Hodder and Stoughton Paperbacks, a division of Hodder and Stoughton Limited, Mill Road, Dunton Green, Sevenoaks, Kent TN13 2YA (Editorial Office: 47 Bedford Square, London WC1B 3DP) by Richard Clay Limited, Bungay, Suffolk.

I

THERE is a reason why I came back to this place—came back here instead of to Canelli, Barbaresco or Alba. It is almost certain that I was not born here; where I was born I don't know. There is not a house or a bit of ground or a handful of dust hereabouts of which I can say: "This was me before I was born." I do not know whether I come from the hills or from the valleys, from the woods or from a great house with a balcony. Maybe the girl who laid me on the cathedral steps in Alba didn't come from the country either—maybe her people had a big house in town; anyhow I was carried there in the kind of basket they use at the grape harvest by two poor women from Monticello or Neive, or perhaps from Cravanzana, why not? Who knows whose flesh and blood I am? I have knocked about the world enough to know that one lot of flesh and blood is as good as another. But that's why you get tired and try to put down roots. To find somewhere where you belong so that you are worth more than the usual round of the seasons and last a bit longer.

If I grew up in this village it is thanks to Virgilia and Padrino—who are both gone now—even if the only reason they reared me was because the orphanage at

5

Alessandria gave them so much a month. For forty years or so ago there were peasants hereabouts so poor that they took in bastards from an orphanage over and above the children they had already, simply to see a silver coin in their hands. Some people took a baby girl so that afterwards they would have a little servant whom they could order about better. Virgilia wanted me because she had two girls already and they hoped when I was a little older to settle down on a big farm where they would all work together and be well off. At that time Padrino had the croft at Gaminella—two rooms and a stable—the goat and the bank covered with hazels. I grew up there with the girls and we used to steal each other's polenta and sleep on the same palliasse. The elder one, Angiolina, was a year older than me and only when I was ten, during the winter when Virgilia died, did I learn by pure chance that I was not her brother. After that winter Angiolina, who was the sensible one, had to stop running about with us along the river bank and in the woods; she looked after the house and made the bread and the cheese. She it was who went to the town hall to draw the money for me. I used to boast to Giulia that I was worth five lire and told her she didn't bring in anything. Then I would ask Padrino why we didn't take in more bastards.

By now I realised that we were miserably poor, for only the poor brought up bastards from the orphanage. At first when they shouted bastard at me as I ran to school, I thought it was a word like coward or beggar and called them names. But although I was already a grown boy and the municipality didn't pay us any more money,

I still didn't quite understand that not to be the son of Padrino and Virgilia meant that I had not been born in Gaminella and had not come from under the hazels or from our goat's ear like the girls.

Last year, the first time I came back to the village, I went almost stealthily to look at the hazels again. The hill at Gaminella was a long slope covered as far as the eye could see with vineyards and terraces, a slant so gradual that if you looked up you could not see the top— and on the top, somewhere, there are other vineyards and other woods and paths—this hill, then, looked as if it had been flayed by the winter and showed up the bareness of the earth and of the tree trunks. In the wintry light I saw its great mass falling gradually away towards Canelli, where our valley finishes. Along the rough country road which follows the Belbo I came to the parapet of the little bridge and to the reed-bed. I saw on the bank the wall of the cottage with its huge blackened stones, the twisted fig-tree and the gaping window and I thought of the terrible winters there. But round about it the face of the land and the trees were changed; the clump of hazels had disappeared and our closely cut patch of millet grass grown smaller. From the byre an ox lowed and in the cold evening air I smelt the manure heap. So the man who had the croft now was not so badly off as we had been. I had always expected something like this or perhaps even that the cottage would have collapsed; I had imagined myself so often on the parapet of the bridge wondering how I could possibly have spent so many years in this hole, walking these few paths, taking the goat to pasture and looking for apples which had

7

rolled down the bank, sure that the world ended where the road overhung the Belbo. But I had not expected not to find the hazels any more. That was the end of everything. These changes made me so cast down that I didn't call out or go on to the threshing floor. There and then I understood what it meant not to be born in a place, not to have it in my blood and be already half-buried there along with my forebears so that any change of crops didn't matter much. Of course there were some clumps of the same hazels on the hillsides and I could still find them, but if *I* had been the owner of this stretch of river bank I would rather have cleared it and sown it with grain; as it was, it had the same effect on me as those rooms you rent in the city, where you live for a day—or for a year—and then when you move on they stay bare and empty shells; they are not really yours, they are dead.

It was a good job that in the evening I turned my back on Gaminella and had in front of me the ridges of the hill at Salto on the other side of the Belbo with its broad meadows which tapered away towards the summit. And lower on this hill, too, there were stretches of trees, and the paths and the scattered farms were there as I had seen them day in, day out, year in, year out, sitting on the beam behind the cottage or on the parapet of the bridge.

Then all these years until I was called up—when I was a hand on the farm they call La Mora, in the rich plain beyond Belbo, and when Padrino had sold his croft at Gaminella and gone with the girls to Cossano—I had only to raise my eyes from the fields to see the vineyards high up on Salto and the way they sloped gradually down towards Canelli, towards the railway and the whistle of the train which ran along by the Belbo morning and evening, making me think of wonders, of stations and cities.

Thus it was that for a long time I thought this village where I had not been born was the whole world. Now that I have really seen the world and know that it is made up of a whole lot of little villages, I am not sure that I was so far wrong when I was a boy. You wander over land and sea just as the lads who were young with me used to go to the festas in the villages round about and dance and drink and fight and bring home flags and barked knuckles. Or you grow grapes and sell them at Canelli; or gather truffles and take them to Alba. There is Nuto, my friend from Salto, who supplies all the valley as far as Cannio with wooden buckets and wine-presses. What does it all mean then? That you need a village, if only for the pleasure of leaving it. Your own village means that you are not alone, that you know there's something of you in the people and the plants and the soil, that even when you are not there it waits to welcome you. But it isn't easy to stay there quietly. For a year now I have had an eye on it and have taken a trip out there from Genoa whenever I could; but it still evades me. Time and experience teach you these things. Is it possible that at forty, after all my travelling, I still don't know what it is to have a village?

There's one thing I can't get used to. Everyone here thinks I have come back to buy a house for myself and they call me the American and show off their daughters. This ought to please a man who left without even a name, and indeed it does. But it isn't enough. I like Genoa, too; I like to know that the world is round, and to have one foot on the gangway. From the time when, as a boy, I leant on my spade at the farm-gate at La Mora and listened to the chatter of people who had nothing better to do as they passed by on the main road—ever since that time, for me, the little hills round Canelli are doors opening on the world. Nuto, who, compared with me, has never been far from Salto, says that if you want to make a life of it in the valley you mustn't ever leave it. Yet he's the one who, when he was still a young lad, got the length of playing the clarinet in the band beyond Canelli and as far away even as Spigno and Ovada, over there where the sun rises. We speak about it from time to time and he laughs.

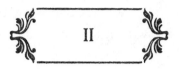

II

THIS SUMMER I put up at the Albergo dell'Angelo in the village square, where no one knew me any more, I have grown so big and fat. And I didn't know anyone in the village either; in my time we came there very seldom, for we stayed on the roads or in the dry watercourses or on the threshing-floor. The village lies very far up the valley, and the Belbo flows in front of the church a good half-hour before it widens out at the foot of the hills where I live.

I had come to have a rest for a fortnight or so and it happened to be the Feast of the Assumption. So much the better, for the comings and goings of strangers and the confusion and uproar in the square would have made even a nigger hard to pick out. I heard them shouting and singing and playing and as darkness fell there were fires and squibs; they drank and jeered and walked in processions and all night for three nights they kept up the dancing in the square, and from it there rose the sound of roundabouts and horns and the crack of air-guns. The very noises, the very wine, the very faces, of long ago. The little boys who ran about among the people's feet were the same; the scarves, the yokes of oxen, the women with stockings on their sunburnt legs, the scent and the sweat, all these were the same. And so was the happiness and the tragedy and the promises made on the banks of the Belbo. The difference was that once upon a time, with my first pay in my hand, I had flung myself into the festivities, at the shooting-booth and on the swings, and we had made the little girls with pigtails cry and none of us boys knew yet why men and women, sleek-headed young men and girls in their pride, met each other and chose each other, laughed in each other's faces and danced together. The difference was that now I knew why they did it—and that these days were past. I had left the valley when I had just begun to understand. Nuto who had stayed, Nuto the joiner at Salto, my accomplice in our first escapades at Canelli, had already played the clarinet for ten years at all the high days and holidays, at all the dances in the valley. For him the world had been a round of festivities these ten years back; he knew all the hard drinkers and all the mountebanks and all the village gaiety.

This last year, every time I've tried to get away from things I've looked him up. His house stands half-way up the side of Salto and looks on to the highway; there is a smell of newly sawn wood there, of flowers and shavings which, in my first days at La Mora, seemed to belong to another world because I came from a poor cottage with a threshing-floor—a smell which meant the main road and the bands and the big houses at Canelli where I had never been yet.

Now Nuto is married and a grown man; he works himself and has men working for him but his house is still the same, and in the sunshine it smells of oleanders and geraniums, for he has pots of them in the windows and in front of the house. The clarinet is hung on the end of the cupboard; underfoot are the shavings which they throw in bucketfuls into a watercourse at the foot of Salto —a watercourse full of acacia and ferns and elders, always dry in summer.

Nuto tells me that he had to make up his mind either to be a joiner or to play in the band, and so after ten years of festas he laid aside the clarinet on the death of his father. When I told him where I had been he said that he had already had news of me from some people from Genoa, and that in the village they told a tale that before I left I had found a pot of gold under the pier of the bridge.

We joked about it. "Now perhaps," I said, "even my father will come to light."

"Your father—*you* are your father," he said.

"In America there's one good thing—they're all bastards."

"That's another thing that should be put right," replied Nuto. "Why should there be people who have no name or home? Aren't we all human beings?"

"Leave things as they are. I got there even without a name."

"*You* have got there," said Nuto, "and no one dare taunt you with it any more; but what about those who haven't? You don't know what a lot of poor devils there still are hereabouts. When I went round with the band, on every doorstep there were idiots and half-wits and byblows, children of drunkards and ignorant servant-girls, forced to live on crusts and cabbage-stalks. Some people even made fun of them. You managed it," said Nuto, "because for good or ill, you found a home, you ate very little at Padrino's, but you did eat. There's no use telling others to make good—we've got to help them."

I like speaking to Nuto; we are men now and we know each other, but long ago in these days at La Mora, when I worked on the farm, he was three years older than I was and knew already how to whistle and play the guitar; his opinion was sought after and listened to; he argued with grown men and with us boys and he winked at the women. Even then I was always at his heels and sometimes played truant to go along the watercourse with him or even in the Belbo to look for nests. He told me what to do if I wanted to be thought well of at La Mora and then in the evening he came into the courtyard and sat late talking with the farm-hands.

And now he was telling me of his life in the band. Round about us were the villages where he had been; by day they shone in the sunlight, picked out by clumps of trees, by night they were nests of stars in the black sky. When he and the rest of the band, whom he taught on Saturday nights in a shed at the station, arrived at the fair, they were full of high spirits; then for the next two or three days they never shut an eye and they stopped playing only to eat—away went the clarinet for the glass, the glass for the fork, then back they went to clarinet or cornet or trumpet. Then they ate a bit more and drank a bit more, then came a solo and after that a snack and then a huge supper, and they'd stay awake till morning. There were festas, processions and marriages, and contests with the rival bands. On the morning of the second and third days they got down from the platform with their eyes popping out of their heads and it was a relief to dash their faces in a bucket of water and maybe throw themselves flat on the meadow grass among the carts and wagons and the droppings of the horses and oxen.

"Who paid for all this?" I used to say. The local authorities, a rich family perhaps, or an ambitious man, all these footed the bill. And those who came to eat, he said, were always the same.

And you should have heard what they ate. I kept remembering the suppers they told about at La Mora, suppers of other villages and other times. But the dishes they served were still the same, and when I heard about them I seemed to be back in the farm-kitchen at La Mora and to see the women busy grating and making the *pasta* and stuffing and lifting the lids off and blowing up the fire, and the taste of it all came back to me, and I heard again the crackling of the broken vine shoots.

"You loved it," I said to him. "Why did you give it up? Because your father died?"

And Nuto said that, first of all, playing doesn't put much in your pocket, and you end by being fed-up with all this waste and never being quite sure who pays for it.

"Then there was the war," he said. "The girls' feet still itched to dance, I suppose, but who was there to dance with them now? People found other ways of amusing themselves in the war years.

"Still, I like music," went on Nuto, thinking it over, "it's only a pity it's a bad master. It gets to be a bad habit and you have to give it up. My father used to say that it was worse than running after women."

"Ah, yes," I said to him, "how have you got on with the women? You liked them once. You see them all at the dancing."

Nuto has a way of laughing and whistling together even when he is being serious.

"You haven't produced anything for the orphanage at Alessandria?"

"I hope not," he said. "For every one like you, how many poor little devils there are."

Then he told me that, of the two, he preferred music. Sometimes they would get together at nights when they were coming home late, and play and play, he and the man with the cornet and the one with the mandoline, going along the main road in the dark far from houses, far from women, far from the dogs who replied with frantic barking, just playing.

"I've never serenaded anyone," he said. "If a girl is pretty, it's not music she's looking for. She wants to cut a figure in front of the other girls—it's a man she's after. I've never met a girl yet who could see the point of music."

Nuto noticed that I was laughing and said quickly, "I'll tell you something: I had an oboe-player, Arboreto, who played so many serenades that we used to say about him 'It's not love they make, these two, it's music.' "

This is how we talked on the main road, or drinking a glass of wine at his window, and below us lay the valley of the Belbo, and the aspens which marked its course and, in front, the great hill at Gaminella, all vineyards and overgrown watercourses. How long was it since I had drunk this wine?

"Have I told you yet," I said to Nuto, "that Cola wants to sell?"

"Only the land?" he said. "Watch he doesn't sell you the bed as well."

"Is it a palliasse or a feather bed?" I said through my teeth. "I am old."

"All the feather beds turn into old sacks," replied Nuto. Then he said, "Have you been to look at La Mora yet?"

That was it—I hadn't been there. It was only a few steps from the house at Salto and I hadn't gone. I knew that the old man and his daughters and the boys and the farm-hands were all scattered, all gone, some dead, some far away. Only Nicoletto was left, that half-witted young nephew of his, who had called bastard after me so often, treading on my toes—and half the stuff was sold.

"One day I'll go. I'm back now," I said.

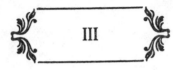

III

OF NUTO and his music I had had news in America, of all places—how long ago was it?—when I still had no intention of coming back, when I'd chucked the railway squad and had arrived in California, travelling from station to station, and when I saw these long slopes in the sunshine, I had said, "I'm home now." Even America came to an end in the sea and this time there was no sense in taking ship again so I stopped among the pine trees and the vineyards. "If they saw me at home with my hoe in my hand, how they would laugh." But they don't use a hoe in California. They're more like gardeners. I met some Piedmontese and I was fed up; it wasn't worth while travelling across so much of the world only to see people like myself who looked at me askance besides. So I cleared out of the country districts and got a job as a milkman at Oakland. In the evening, across the waters of the bay you could see the lights of San Francisco. I went there and starved for a month, and when I came out of prison I was at the stage where I envied the Chinese. By this time I wondered if it was worth while travelling round the world to see anyone. I went back to the hills.

I had been living there for a bit and I had got a girl whom I didn't like any longer now that she worked in the same joint as myself. Because she'd come so often to meet me at the door, she'd been taken on as cashier and now all day she gazed at me over the counter while I fried the bacon and filled the glasses. In the evening I left the shop and she came to meet me, running along the pavement in her high heels, and wanting us to stop a car to go down to the sea or to go to the cinema. The moment we were away from the light of the eating-house, we were alone in the starlight among the din of the cicalas and frogs. I wished I could have taken her into the fields among the apple trees and the clumps of wood or even among the short grass on the roadsides and thrown her down on the earth and given some meaning to all the uproar under the stars. She wasn't having any. She shrieked like women do and wanted to go to another joint. Before you could lay hands on her—we had a room in a side-street in Oakland—she had to be tight.

It was one of these nights that I heard about Nuto. From a man who came from Bubbio. I recognised him by his build and his walk before he even opened his mouth. He was driving a lorry-load of timber and while they were filling up his petrol tanks outside he asked me for a beer.

"A bottle of wine would be better," I said in our dialect, my lips pressed tight together.

His eyes laughed and he looked at me. We talked all evening, until they'd nearly broken his horn outside. From the till, Nora listened with all her ears and began to fidget, but Nora had never been in Alessandria and she didn't understand. In the end, I even poured my friend out a glass of bootleg whiskey. He told me he'd been a lorry-driver at home and the names of the villages he'd gone round and why he'd come to America. "But if I'd known that they drink this sort of stuff. . . . There's no denying, it warms you up, but there's no wine hereabouts."

"There's nothing here," I said. "It's like living on the moon."

Nora was annoyed and was tidying her hair. She turned round on her chair and got some dance music on the wireless. My friend shrugged his shoulders and bent over the counter, pointing over his shoulder. "Do you like these women?" he asked.

I gave the counter a rub. "It's our own fault," I said. "This is where they belong."

He said nothing and listened to the wireless. I heard through the music the sound of the frogs; it never altered. Nora squared her shoulders and looked contemptuously at his back.

"It's just like this music of theirs," he said. "There's no comparison. They don't know how to play at all."

And he told me about the competition at Nizza the year before, when the bands had come from all the villages round about, the band from Cortemilia and San Marzano and Canelli and Neive and they had played and played so that people just stood and listened and they had had to put off the horse-races, and even the priest listened to the dance music, and they drank only to be able to play, and at midnight they were still playing and Tiberio and the band from Neive had won. But there had been arguments and fights and bottles broken over people's heads, and according to him Nuto from Salto deserved the prize.

"Nuto? But I know him."

And then this new friend told me who Nuto was now and what he was doing. He told me how on that same night Nuto had wanted to show them a thing or two and had gone along the main road playing on until they came to Calamandrana. This man had followed them on a bicycle in the moonlight and they played so well that the women jumped out of bed and came out of their houses and clapped their hands and then the band stopped and began another tune. Nuto was in the middle and led them on the clarinet.

Nora shouted to me to make them stop hooting. I poured out another glass for my friend and asked him when he was going back to Bubbio.

"I'd go tomorrow," he said, "if I could."

That night, before going home to Oakland, I went and smoked a cigarette on the grass far from the main road where the cars were passing. There was no moon but a sea of stars, as many stars as there were frogs and cicalas. Even if Nora had let me fling her down on the grass that night, it wouldn't have been enough for me. The frogs would have gone on croaking and the cars would have gone hurtling on down the hill, gathering speed, and America would still have finished where the road ended, would still have finished in these brightly lit cities on the coast. In the dark, among the scent of gardens and pine trees, I realised that these stars weren't my stars, and that they frightened me, like Nora and the customers. The bacon and eggs, the good pay, the oranges as big as water-melons went for nothing, they were like the crickets and the frogs. Was it worth while having come?

Where could I go now? Throw myself off the break-water?

Now I understood why every so often a girl was found strangled in a car or in a room or at the end of an alley. Maybe these people, too, wanted to fling themselves down on the grass and be in tune with the frogs and possess a bit of ground the length of a woman and really sleep there and not be afraid. And yet it was a big country, there was enough for everyone. There were women, there was land, there was money. But no one had enough of them, no one ever stopped no matter how much he had and the fields and the vineyards were like public gardens, artificial flower-beds like you see at stations, or else uncultivated parched land, cast-iron mountains. It wasn't a country where a man could settle down and rest his head and say to the others, "Here I am for good or ill. For good or ill let me live in peace." This was what was frightening. The people didn't even know one another; when you crossed the mountains you saw at every turn that no one had ever settled there or put a hand on them. That was why they would beat up a drunk man and put him in prison and leave him for dead. And it wasn't only their drink that was bad but their women, too. Then one fine day one of them wanted to touch something, to make his name, and so he strangled a woman, shot her in her sleep, bashed in her head with a spanner.

Nora called from the road that she wanted to go into town. In the distance her voice sounded like the cicalas. I could hardly keep from laughing at the idea of what she would have said if she had known what I was thinking.

But you don't talk about these things to anyone, there's no point. One fine morning she wouldn't see me any more, that was all. But where could I go? I had got to the end of the world, to its farthest shore, and I had had enough. It was then I began to think I could go back across the mountains.

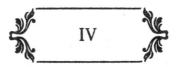

IV

BUT NUTO didn't want to put the clarinet to his mouth, even for the feast of the Assumption in August—he says it's like smoking, when you stop, you must stop altogether. In the evening he came to the Albergo dell'Angelo and we stood on the balcony of my room, enjoying the cool air. The balcony looks on to the piazza and the piazza was like Judgment Day, but we were looking beyond the roofs at the vineyards lying white under the moon.

Nuto, who wants to think out everything for himself, talked to me about the sort of place this world is and wanted me to tell him what people do and what they say, and listened, leaning his chin on the railing.

"If I could play as well as you," I said, "I wouldn't have gone to America. You know how it is at that age. You've only got to see a girl, or start a scrap with someone or come home in the small hours. A man wants to do something, get somewhere, make up his own mind.

You can't bear to live the way you did before. It seems easier to keep moving. You hear so much talk. At that age a village square like this seems the whole world. You think that the world will be like this, too."

Nuto was silent and looked at the roofs.

"Who knows how many boys there are down there," I said, "who would like to take the road to Canelli. . . ."

"But they don't take it," said Nuto. "You took it. Why?"

Is this the sort of thing you can know? Was it because at La Mora they called me Anguilla—the eel? Or because one morning on the bridge at Canelli I saw a car run into an ox? Or because I didn't even know how to play the guitar?

"At La Mora," I said, "I was too comfortable. I thought the whole world was like La Mora."

"No," said Nuto, "they are badly off here, but no one goes away. It's because it's their fate. But you—in Genoa, in America—obviously you had to do something on your own, find out your own fate."

"My own fate? But I didn't need to go as far as that."

"But maybe you're in luck," said Nuto. "You've made money, haven't you? Maybe you haven't even noticed it. But something's bound to happen to everyone."

While he spoke he kept his head down and his voice echoed, distorted, from the railing. He ran his teeth along it. He seemed to be playing a game. All of a sudden he raised his head.

"Some day I'll tell you about what happened here," he said. "We all have our own luck. There'll be a handful of boys, they aren't anybody in particular, they aren't doing any harm, but one fine day, they start to . . ."

I could see he spoke with difficulty. He swallowed hard. Since we'd met again I hadn't got used yet to thinking of him as any different from that scamp of a Nuto who was so much all there that he went about putting people right and always had something to say for himself. It never occurred to me that now I had caught up on him and one knew as much as the other. He didn't even seem changed—he was only a bit more solid, a bit less of a dreamer. That cat's face of his was quieter and more surly. I waited for him to pluck up his courage and get rid of what was on his mind. I've always found that people tell you everything, if you give them time.

But that night Nuto didn't get it off his chest. He changed the subject and said, "Just listen to them jumping about and blaspheming. To get them to come and pray to the Madonna, the priest has to allow them to let off steam. And before they can let off steam, they have to burn a candle to the Madonna. Who cheats who?"

"They cheat each other time about," I said.

"No, no," said Nuto, "the priest has the best of it. Who pays for the lights and fireworks, and the stipend and the music? And who can still laugh the day after the festa? Poor devils, they break their backs working their patch of ground and then let everything be taken off them."

"But don't the families who want to get on in the world pay the most?"

"And where do these families get the money? They make their farm-hands work and their maids and their peasants. And their land, where did they get it? Why should some people have everything and the others nothing?"

"What are you? A communist?"

Nuto looked at me with a wry smile. He let the band have a good blow and then muttered, looking at me closely all the time: "We don't know enough in this village. It's not communists you want. There was a man, Ghigna we called him, who said he was a communist and sold peppers in the piazza. He used to get drunk and then he shouted all night. People like that do more harm than good. What we need are communists who aren't ignorant, who don't disgrace the name of communism. Ghigna—they soon fixed him, no one bought his peppers any more. He had to go away this winter."

I said he was right but they should have done something in 1945 when the iron was hot. And then even Ghigna would have been a help. I thought when I came back to Italy I'd find something done. You had the whip hand.

"I'd only a plane and a chisel," said Nuto.

"I've seen poverty everywhere," I said. "There are villages where the flies fare better than human beings. But they're not badly enough off to revolt. The people need to be driven to it. In those days you had been driven to it and you had the power. Were you out on the hills, too?"

I had never asked him before. Several people in the village—young lads who had come into the world when we weren't twenty yet—had told me how men had died on these roads and in these woods. I knew a lot and I'd asked him about things but I hadn't asked if he had worn the red scarf and carried a gun. I knew these woods had been full of strangers, men who had refused to be called up, who had got clear of the city, hot-heads all of them, and Nuto wasn't one of these. But Nuto is Nuto and knows better than I do what is right.

"No," said Nuto, "if I'd gone, they'd have burnt my house."

Nuto had kept a wounded partisan hidden in a hole in the gully on Salto and carried food to him at night. His mother had told me about it and I wasn't surprised. It was just like Nuto. Only yesterday when he met two boys on the road who were tormenting a lizard, he took it from them. We are all twenty years older.

"If Sor Matteo had done it to us when we ran about in the watercourse"—I had said to him—"what would you have said? How many nests did you harry in your time?"

"It's a stupid thing to do," he said. "We were both in the wrong. Let the beasts live. They have a hard enough time of it in the winter."

"I'm not arguing with you—you're quite right."

"And then if they start off like this, they end off by cutting throats and burning villages."

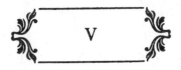

V

THE SUN is fierce up in these hills; I had forgotten how its light is flung back off the bare patches of volcanic rock. Here the heat doesn't so much come down from the sky as rise up underfoot—from the earth, from the trench between the vines which seems to have devoured each speck of green and turned it to stem. I like this heat, it has a smell, and I'm a part of the smell—there are so many grape-harvests in it, so many hay-harvests, so many piles of stripped leaves, so many tastes, and so many desires that I didn't know I had any longer. And so I like to come out of the Albergo dell'Angelo and look at the land; I almost wish I hadn't lived the life I have and could change it, could say there is some truth in the gossip of the people who see me pass by and wonder if I've come to buy grapes or what. Here in the village no one remembers me any more, no one holds it against me that I have been a farm-hand and a bastard. They know that I have money in Genoa. Maybe there's a boy, a farm-hand like I was, a woman wearying behind drawn blinds, who thinks of me as I used to think of the little hills at Canelli, of the people down there in the big world, who make money and have a fine time of it and go far across the sea.

As for farms, several people have already offered them to me, half-joking, half-serious. I stand there and listen with my hands behind my back—not all of them know I'm up in these things—and they tell me about the big harvests of the last four years, but now they would need some trenching done, or a wall built, or a vine transplanted and they can't do it.

"Where are these harvests?" I ask them. "Where are these profits? Why didn't you spend them on the land?"

"It all went on manures. . . ."

And I cut them short—I've sold manures wholesale. But I enjoy talking to them. And I enjoy it even more if we go through the fields, when we walk over a threshing-floor or look in at a stable or drink a glass of wine.

The day I went back to the croft at Gaminella, I'd met old Valino already. Nuto had stopped him in the square when I was with him and asked him if he knew me. He was dark and thin, with eyes like a mole which looked at me narrowly, and when Nuto told him laughing that here was someone who had eaten his bread and drunk his wine, his face clouded and he stood there without committing himself. Then I asked him if he'd been the one who'd cut down the hazels and if there was still that trellis of little grapes over the stable. We told him who I was and where I came from, but Valino didn't take the black look off his face and said only that the land was poor on the hillside and the rains took away a bit more every year. Before he left us, he looked at me and he looked at Nuto and said: "Come up some time. I want you to look at that vat of mine that's leaking."

Then Nuto had said to me, "You didn't eat every day

in Gaminella.'' He wasn't joking any longer. ''But you didn't have to share the crop. Now the Signora at the villa has bought the croft and comes with her scales to divide out the harvests. She's a woman with two big farms and a business over and above. And then they say 'The peasants rob us and work against us'.''

I came back along that road alone and thought about the sort of life that Valino would have led all these years —sixty, was it? perhaps not even that—that he'd been working and paying half his rent in kind. How many houses had he left, how many bits of land, after he'd slept there and eaten there, and hoed the earth in the heat and the cold, carrying his belongings on a cart which was not even his over roads he would never tread again. I knew he was a widower, for his wife had died in the farm before this one and his eldest sons had been killed in the war—he had nothing left except a young boy and his womenfolk. What else was he here for?

He had never got out of the valley of the Belbo. Without meaning to, I came to a stop on the path and thought that if I hadn't run away twenty years before, this would have been my fate, too. And yet I have gone on wandering about the world and he has wandered over these hills without ever being able to say ''This land belongs to me. On this bench I shall grow old. In this room I shall die.''

I came to the fig tree in front of the threshing-floor and saw again the path between the two grassy banks. They had put stones down now to make steps. The slope from the meadow to the road was just the same as it used to be, dry grass below the heap of brushwood, a broken basket, some squashed apples going bad. Up above I heard the farm dog running backwards and forwards along the wire to which its lead was attached.

When my head appeared at the top of the steps, the dog went mad. It jumped about and howled and nearly throttled itself. I went on up the path and saw the porch and the trunk of the fig tree and a rake propped against the door—the same rope with the knot in it was hanging from the latch. The same stain of copper-sulphate was round the vine-trellis. The same bush of rosemary was at the corner of the house. And there was the smell, the smell of the house, of the watercourse, of rotten apples and dry grass and rosemary.

There was a wheel lying on the ground and a boy sitting on it wearing a shirt and ragged trousers held up by broken braces; he had one of his legs stretched out, kept apart from the other in a way that wasn't natural. Was this a game he was playing? He looked at me standing there in the sunshine; in his hand he had a dried rabbit-skin and he closed his thin eyelids to gain time.

I stopped and he kept blinking his eyes; the dog howled and tore at the wire. The boy was barefoot; he had a scab under one eye and bony shoulders and he kept his leg still.

I suddenly remembered how often I had had chilblains and scabs on my knee and cracked lips. I remembered I wore clogs only in winter. I remembered how mother Virgilia stripped the skin from rabbits when she had gutted them. I raised my hand and beckoned to him.

On the doorstep a woman had appeared, two women in black skirts; one was decrepit and twisted, one was younger and skinny and both were looking at me. I shouted that I was looking for Valino. He wasn't there, he had gone up by the gully.

The one who wasn't so old shouted to the dog and took hold of the wire and pulled it until the dog choked. The boy got up from the wheel—he got up with a struggle, sticking out his leg to one side and when he was on his feet he trailed over towards the dog. He was lame and he had rickets and I saw that his knee wasn't any thicker than his arm and he dragged his foot behind him like a weight. He would be about ten years old and to see him on that threshing-floor was like seeing myself. So much so that I took a quick look under the porch, behind the fig tree, towards the millet patch in case Angiolina and Giulia would appear. I wondered where they were. If they were still alive somewhere or other, they must be about the age of that woman there.

When the dog had quietened down, they didn't speak, but stood looking at me.

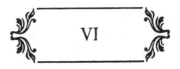

VI

Then I said I would wait for Valino if he was coming back. They answered together that he was late sometimes.

The one who had tied up the dog—she was barefoot and burnt with the sun, and, there were no two ways about it, she had the makings of a beard—looked at me with Valino's dark and wary eyes. She was the sister-in-law and slept with him now and she'd come to look like him, being constantly with him.

I went on to the threshing-floor (the dog hurled itself at me again) and said I'd been a little boy here. I asked them if the well was still at the back. The old woman was sitting on the door-step now and muttering uneasily; the other bent down and picked up the rake which had fallen in front of the door, then she called to the boy to give a look from the edge of the gully to see if he saw his Dad. Then I said there was no need, I'd been passing down below there and I'd suddenly wanted to have another look at the house where I'd grown up, but I knew all the fields and the gully as far as the walnut tree and I could wander around by myself and see if there was anyone about.

Then I asked: "What's wrong with this boy? Did he fall on a hoe?"

The two women looked from me to him and he began to laugh—he laughed soundlessly and all at once he closed his eyes tightly. I knew this trick, too.

"What's wrong with you?" I said. "What's your name?"

It was the thin sister-in-law who answered me. She said the doctor had looked at Cinto's leg the year Mentina died when they were still at Orto—Mentina lay in bed groaning and the day before she died the doctor had told her it was her fault the boy hadn't good bones. Mentina had answered that the other sons who had been killed in the war were all right but this one was born like that, she knew the mad dog that tried to bite her would make her lose her milk. The doctor had answered her roughly and said it wasn't the milk at all but the bundles of brushwood, walking barefoot in the rain, eating lentils and polenta, and carrying baskets. She should have thought of that long ago, the doctor had said, but now it was too late. And Mentina had answered that the others had been all right anyway, and the next day she was dead.

The boy listened to us, leaning against the wall and I noticed that he wasn't really laughing—his jaws protruded and his teeth were set far apart and he had this scab under one eye—he seemed to be laughing but instead he was taking it all in.

I said to the women, "And now I'm going to look for Valino." I wanted to be alone. But the women shouted at the boy, "Get a move on. You go and look, too."

So I went through the meadow and along the side of the vineyard which was stubble now between the rows of vines, baked by the sun. Although the hillside behind the vineyard, instead of the dark shadow of the hazels, was a low field of millet now, so low that you could see right over it, the bit of country you saw was a mere scrap the size of a handkerchief. Cinto limped along behind me and in a moment we were at the walnut tree. I couldn't imagine I'd run about and played so much between here and the road or climbed down into the gully to find walnuts or fallen apples or spent whole afternoons with the girls and the goat there on the grass, or waited in the winter days for a blink of sunshine to be able to go out again—it didn't seem possible even if this had been a country or the whole world. If I hadn't happened to get out of here when I was thirteen and Padrino went to stay at Cossano, I would still be living the same life as Valino or Cinto. It was a mystery to me how we had been able to scrape together enough to eat. We nibbled at apples and pumpkins and chick peas and Virgilia managed to take the edge off our hunger. But now I understood the black look on Valino's face, who worked and worked and still had to divide the fruits of his labours. You could see the results of it—two savage women and a crippled boy.

I asked Cinto if he'd been old enough to remember the hazels. Balanced on his good foot, he stared at me incredulously and said there were still a few trees at the bottom of the gully. When I turned round to speak to him I saw over the vines the dark woman watching us from the threshing-floor. I was ashamed of my suit and my shirt and my shoes. How long was it since I had gone barefoot. To convince Cinto that I'd been like him once, I had to do more than just talk about Gaminella. For him

Gaminella was the whole world and they all spoke to him as if it were. What would I have said in my day if a big fellow like myself had appeared before me and I had gone round the farm with him? For a moment I had the illusion that the girls and the goat would be waiting for me at the house and that I would have boasted to them about it.

Cinto was interested now and followed me about. I took him to the far end of the vineyard. I didn't recognise the rows of vines any longer and I asked him who had done the transplanting. He gossiped and put on airs and told me that the Signora from the villa had come along yesterday to gather the tomatoes.

"Did she leave you any?" I asked.

"We'd put them by already," he said.

Where we were, behind the vineyard, there was still grass and the goat's drinking-trough and then the hill went on above us. I got him to tell me who stayed in the houses in the distance and I told him I used to stay here once and what kind of dogs I had, and said that we were all boys then. He listened to me and said that some of them were still there. Then I asked him if there was still that chaffinch's nest on the tree which rose out of the gully at our feet. I asked him if he ever went into the Belbo to fish with the basket.

It was strange how everything was changed and yet the same. Not even a vineshoot remained from the old stocks, not even a beast; now the meadows were stubble and the stubble fields were vineyards and the people had moved on and grown up and died; the roots had come away and the trees had rolled down into the Belbo—and yet when I looked round at the great shoulder of

Gaminella, the distant paths on the hill at Salto, the threshing-floors, the wells, the voices and the hoes, everything was just the same, everything had the taste, the smell, the colour of long ago.

I made him tell me if he knew the villages round about. If he had ever been to Canelli. He had been on the cart when his Dad went to sell the grapes at Gancia. And some days they crossed the Belbo with the boys from Piola and went on to the railway line to see the trains pass.

I told him that in my time this valley was bigger, there were people who drove about it in a carriage and the men had a golden chain hanging from their waistcoats, and the women from the village, from the Station, carried parasols. I told him that they held festivals—weddings, baptisms, all the festivals of the Madonna—and people came from far away, from as far as the end of the hills, men who played in the band, hunters and village mayors. There were houses—big houses, like the one they call Il Nido on the hill at Canelli—which had rooms that held fifteen or twenty at a time, like the Albergo dell'Angelo, and they ate and played all day. And we boys, too, had our own celebrations on the threshing-floors and we played at a kind of hopscotch in summer and in winter we spun tops on the ice. We played hopscotch by jumping on one leg, the way he was standing, over rows of pebbles without touching them. After the grape harvest the hunters went all over the hills and through the woods, and went up past Gaminella and San Grato and Camo, and came back muddy and dead tired but laden with partridges, hares and other game. From the croft we saw them passing and then we heard them making merry until nightfall in the village houses and in Il Nido down there— at that time we could see quite well, for these trees weren't there—all the windows were lit up as if they were on fire, and we saw the shadows of the guests passing to and fro until morning.

Cinto listened with his mouth wide open and the scab under his eye, sitting against the bank.

I was a boy like you, I said to him, and I lived here with Padrino and we had a goat. I took it to graze. In winter when there were no more hunters about, it wasn't much fun, because we couldn't even go up the gully, there was so much water and ice and once the wolves—there are none now—couldn't find any more to eat in the woods and they came down from Gaminella, and in the morning we saw their footprints in the snow. They look like dogs' footprints but they're deeper. I slept in the room at the back with the girls and at nights we used to hear the wolf moaning because it was cold in the gully.

"There was a dead man in the gully last year," said Cinto.

I stopped and asked what dead man.

"A German," he said, "that the partisans had buried in Gaminella. All the skin had come off."

"As close to the road as that?" I asked.

"No, he came from up there, from the gully. The water brought him down and my Dad found him under the mud and stones."

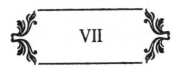

VII

MEANWHILE from the gully came the noise of a bill-hook jarring on wood and, at each blow, Cinto blinked.

"It's my Dad," he said. "He's down there."

I asked him why he kept his eyes shut at first while I was looking at him and the women were speaking. Suddenly he closed them again instinctively and said he hadn't. I began to laugh and said I'd played at that game, too, when I was a boy—I saw only what I wanted to see and when I opened them again, I had fun seeing what everything was really like.

Then he was pleased and bared his teeth and said the rabbits did like this, too.

"That German," I said, "will have been all eaten up by ants."

A shout from the woman on the threshing-floor, calling Cinto, wanting Cinto, cursing Cinto, made us smile. You often hear a voice like that on the hills.

"You couldn't make out any more how they had killed him," he said. "He'd been buried for two winters."

When we slid down through the thick leaves and the brambles and the mint in the bottom of the gully, Valino scarcely lifted his head. He was busy polling the red branches of a willow with the bill-hook. While outside the watercourse it was August, down here it was cold and half-dark, as usual. Here the water had come down once and lay in a pool in summer. I asked him where he put the withies to season this year (it had been so dry). He bent to lift up his bundle of branches, then changed his mind. He stood and looked at me, one foot on the bundle, and hitching the bill-hook to the back of his trousers. He wore the splashed trousers and hat (they were almost sky-blue) that they wear for spraying the grapes.

"The grapes are good this year," I said, "you only need a bit more water."

"There's always something we want," said Valino. "I was looking for Nuto about that vat. Is he not coming?"

Then I explained I'd happened to be passing on my way from Gaminella and had wanted to see the old place again. I hardly recognised it, there had been so much work put out on it. The vineyard was freshly planted three years ago, wasn't it? And had they done a lot in the house, too? I asked him. When *I* stayed here, there was always that chimney that didn't draw properly, and had they broken down the wall?

Valino said that the women stayed in the house. That was their job. He looked up the gully through the little leaves of the aspens. He said that the land here was like land anywhere else—to get anything out of it, you would have needed hands to work it and they were gone now.

Then we spoke about the war and those who had died. He didn't say anything about his sons. He muttered away. When I spoke about the partisans and the Germans, he shrugged his shoulders. He said he was at Orto then and had seen them burning a house. For a year no one had done any work on the land and if all these men had gone home instead—the Germans to their own homes, the young men to their farms—it would have been a good job. What strange faces, what strange people—they'd never seen so many people from outside before, not even at the fairs when he was a boy.

Cinto stood and listened to us, his mouth wide open. "Who knows," I said, "how many of them are still buried in the woods?"

Valino looked at me, his face dark, his eyes clouded and hard.

"There are some there," he said, "there are some. All you need is the time to look for them." There was no disgust in his voice or pity. It was as if he were speaking about going to look for mushrooms or firewood. His face lit up for a moment, then he said, "No good came of them when they were alive, and none now they're dead."

There you are, I thought, Nuto would have called him a stupid lout and asked him if the world was always to be the same. Nuto who had seen so many villages and knew the poverty of all these round about, Nuto would never have asked what use the war had been. We had to fight it, that was our fate. Nuto has got this idea on the brain, that something which has got to happen is everybody's business, and the world is a botched job and needs remaking.

Valino didn't ask me to come up to the house with him and have a glass of wine. He picked up the bundle of withies again and asked Cinto if he had cut the green stuff for the rabbits. Cinto moved away and looked down without replying. Then Valino stepped forward and with his free hand took a cut at him with a willow branch. Cinto leapt away and Valino stumbled and got his footing again. Cinto, back in the gully, was looking at him now. Without speaking he set off up the side of the hill, the withies in his arms. He didn't turn round even when he was at the top. I felt like a boy come to play with Cinto— the old man had lifted his hand to him because he couldn't do it to me. Cinto and I looked at each other and laughed without speaking.

We came down the gully under the cool vault of the trees, but we had only to pass the unshaded pools to feel the sultry heat and the sweat. I was looking at the stone wall, the one opposite our meadow, which shored up the vineyard at Il Morone. At the top, above the brambles, you could see the first bright green vine shoots and a fine peach tree, some of its leaves already red, just like the one that was there in my time with the peaches that fell into the gully and seemed better than our own. These apple trees and peach trees which have red and yellow leaves in summer, make my mouth water even now, because the leaf looks like a ripe fruit and it's a joy to stand beneath the tree. For my part, I'd like all trees to bear fruit, that's the way it is in the vineyard.

Cinto and I talked about the *pallone* players and then about the card players and we came onto the road under the little bridge over the gully, among the acacias. Cinto had seen a stall-keeper in the piazza with a pack of cards in his hands and told me he had a two of spades at home and a king of hearts that someone had lost on the main road. They were a bit dirty but quite good and if he could find the others as well, they would do. I told him there were some people who played for their living and they staked houses and land.

I had been in a village, I told him, where they played with a pile of golden crowns on the table and a pistol in their waistcoat pocket. And even in our village when I was a boy, after the owners of the big farms had sold their grapes or their grain, they harnessed their horses and set out in the cool of the evening for Nizza or Acqui with bags of golden coins and they played all night long; they staked their money, then their woods, then their fields, and finally their farm, and the morning afterwards they found them dead in their bed at the inn under the picture of the Madonna and the sprig of olive. Or else they went off in their gig and no one heard any more about them. Someone even staked his wife and so the children were left alone; they were chased out of their house and these are the ones who are called bastards.

"Maurino's son is a bastard," said Cinto.

"People take them in," I said to him. "It's always poor people who take in bastards. Maurino must have needed a boy."

"If you say he's one, he flies into a rage," said Cinto.

"You mustn't say it to him. Is it your fault if your father gives you away? All you need is the will to work. I have known bastards who have bought big farms."

We had come out of the gully and Cinto had run on ahead of me and sat down on the parapet. Behind the aspens on the other side of the road was the Belbo. It was here that we would come out to play after the goat had led us a dance over the hillsides and through the gullies all afternoon. The stones on the road were the same and the green trunks of the aspens smelt like running water.

"Aren't you going to cut some green stuff for the rabbits?" I asked.

Cinto said he was just going. Then I set off and I felt his eyes on me from the reeds until I came to the bend in the road.

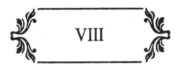

VIII

I MADE up my mind I wouldn't go back to the croft at Gaminella unless Nuto was there, so that Valino would let me into the house. This road is out of Nuto's way, but I passed there often and Cinto would be waiting for me on the path or would emerge from the reeds. He leant against the parapet with his leg sticking out and let me talk away.

But after the first few days when the festa was over and the *pallone* matches, the Albergo dell'Angelo became quiet again and when I drank my coffee at the window with flies buzzing all round me and looked out on the empty square, I felt like a mayor looking down from the balcony of the town hall. I'd never have thought of that when I was a boy. When you're far from home, you work because you have to and you make your fortune without meaning to—to make your fortune means just this, to go far away and come back like me, grown rich and big and fat, and free to do what I wanted. I didn't know this when I was a boy, although I was always gazing at the road and the passers-by and the big houses at Canelli and the hills on the horizon.

"That's the way things are fated to be," said Nuto, who, compared with me, hasn't bestirred himself. He hasn't travelled about the world or made his fortune. What happens to so many in this valley might have happened to him, too—to grow up like a tree, and then to grow old like a woman or a goat, without knowing what happens beyond the Bormida or ever escaping from the round of the house and the grape harvest and the fairs. But even though he hadn't moved about much something had happened to him, too—that idea of his that things must be understood and put right, that the world is badly made and it's everyone's job to change it.

I saw now that even when, as a boy, I chased the goat or broke the bundles of brushwood in a rage in the winter-time by putting my foot on top of them, or shut my eyes to see if the hill had vanished when I opened them again—even then I was preparing myself for what fate had in store for me, to live without a home of my own and always hope that there would be a village fairer and richer beyond the hills. As for this room at the Albergo dell'Angelo—I had never been there then—it seemed as if I had always known that when a signore, a man with his pockets full of gold coins, the owner of big farms, set out in his gig to see the world he'd find himself one fine morning in a room like this and wash his hands in the white basin and write a letter on the old polished table,

45

a letter which would go far away, to the city, and hunters would read it, and mayors and ladies with umbrellas. And here it was happening. In the morning I drank my coffee and wrote letters to Genoa, to America, I handled money, I employed people. Perhaps in a month I would be at sea again, following my letters.

I had coffee one day with the Cavaliere, downstairs, looking out on to the scorching square. The Cavaliere was the son of the old Cavaliere who in my time owned the lands of Il Castello and a whole lot of water-mills and had even built a dyke out in the Belbo when I had still to be born. He passed sometimes along the main road in his carriage and pair driven by his coachman. They had a small country house in the village with a walled garden full of unfamiliar trees, whose name nobody knew. The shutters of the villa were always closed when I ran to school in winter and stopped in front of the iron gate.

Now the old Cavaliere was dead and his son was a little baldheaded lawyer who never meddled with the law; the lands, the houses, the mills, he had got through them all in his bachelor days in the city and the great family of Castello had disappeared. He was left with a little vine-yard and shabby clothes and he went about the village with a silver-topped cane. He started to speak to me very civilly; he knew where I came from and asked me if I had been in France as well, and he drank his coffee crooking his little finger and bending forward.

He stopped every day in front of the inn and talked with the other customers. He knew a lot, more than the young men did, or the doctor or myself, but they were things that didn't fit into the life he led now—you only had to let him talk to see that the old Cavaliere had just died in time. It occurred to me that he was a little like that garden at the villa, full of palms and exotic grasses and flowers with labels. In his own way, the Cavaliere, too, had escaped from the village and travelled about the world, but he hadn't made his fortune. His relations had cut him off, his wife (a countess from Turin) was dead, and his son, his only son, the future Cavaliere, had killed himself, because he'd got into a mess with women and gambling before he even went to do his military service. And yet this old man, this miserable creature, who slept in the same hovel as the peasants who worked his last bit of vineyard, was always polite, always just so, always the gentleman, and raised his hat each time he met me.

From the square you could see the little hill where he had his bit of land, behind the roof of the town hall, a badly kept vineyard full of weeds, and above it, against the sky, a tuft of pines and canes. In the afternoon the group of idlers drinking their coffee often pulled his leg about his peasants who owned half Sam Grato and lived in his house only because it was handy to be so close to the village and never dreamt of hoeing the vineyard. But he replied—and he believed it—that the peasants knew what a vineyard needed and anyhow there had been a time when landed gentry let some of their estate go wild so that they could hunt there, or even for a whim.

They all laughed at the idea of the Cavaliere going hunting, and someone said he would have been better to plant chick peas.

I have planted trees, he said jerkily with unexpected heat and his voice trembled. Being so well-bred, he

47

couldn't stand up for himself and then I put in a word to change the subject. He changed the subject but it was obvious that the old Cavaliere lived on in him, because the old boy had seen what I was getting at. When I got up, he begged a word with me and we walked across the piazza under the gaze of the others. He told me he was old and too much alone and his house wasn't a fit place to receive anyone, but if I came up to pay him a visit, whenever it suited me, he would be very pleased. He knew I had visited others to see the farms, so if I had a moment to spare. . . . I was wrong again; just wait, I said to myself, I bet he wants to sell, too. I replied that I wasn't in the village on business.

"No, no," he said at once. "Just a visit. . . . I want to show you those trees, if you will allow me."

I went right away to save him the trouble of preparing for me and as we went along the path above the dark roofs and the courtyards of the houses he told me that he could not sell the vineyard for many reasons—because it was the last bit of land to bear his name, because, if he sold it, he would die in someone else's house, because it suited his peasants this way, because he was so alone.

"You don't know," he said, "what it means to live in these parts without a morsel of land. Where are your people buried?"

I told him I didn't know. He fell silent for a moment, became animated again, and then bewildered and shook his head.

"I understand," he said softly. "Life's like that."

He, poor devil, had buried someone in the village churchyard not so long ago. Twelve years ago and it seemed like yesterday to him. It hadn't been an ordinary death, the sort of death you get resigned to or can think about without misgivings.

"I've made a lot of stupid mistakes," he said to me. "Everyone does in this life. The real affliction of old age is remorse. But one thing I cannot forgive myself. That boy . . ."

We had come to the bend in the road, under the canes. He stopped and stammered, "You know how he died?"

I nodded. He gripped the knob of his stick as he spoke. "I planted these trees," he said. Behind the canes I could see a pine tree. "I wanted the top of the hill here to be for him, the way he liked it, free and wild like the park where he was a boy."

He had something there. The clump of canes and behind them the reddish pine trees with the rank grass underneath reminded me of the hollow in the hills above the vineyard at Gaminella. But what was striking here was that it was the crest of the hill and there was nothing beyond it.

"Every estate," I said, "should have a bit of land left wild like this. But as for working in the vineyard . . ." I said.

At our feet we saw his four miserable rows of vines. The Cavaliere made a mocking grimace and raised his hat.

"I'm old," he said. "These boors!"

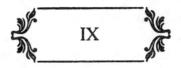

IX

AND NOW I should really have gone down into the courtyard of the house to please him. But I knew that he
would have had to open a bottle of wine for me and then
pay his peasants for it. I said it was late and someone was
waiting for me in the village and at that hour I never
took anything. I left him in his wood under the pine
trees.

I thought over this story every time I passed along the
road from Gaminella, at the reed-bed beside the bridge.
Here I too had played with Angiolina and Giulia and cut
green stuff for the rabbits. Cinto was often at the bridge
because I had given him fish hooks and a line and told
him how you fish out at sea and shoot the seagulls. From
here you don't see either San Grato or the village. But
on the great crests of Gaminella and Salto and on the
more distant hills beyond Canelli there were dark tufts of
trees and reeds and scrub—still the same—just like the
Cavaliere's. When I was a boy I never managed to climb
up as far as that; when I was a young man I was working
and asked no more than to go to the fairs and the dancing.
Now, although I didn't come to any decision, I kept
thinking that there must be something up there, on these
long slopes, behind the canes and the last scattered farms.

What could there be? Up there it was uncultivated and scorched by the sun.

"Have you had the bonfires this year?" I asked Cinto. "We always had them. On St. John's Eve all the hillside was ablaze."

"Little ones," he said. "They make a big one at the Station but you can't see it from here. Piola said that once they burnt bundles of brushwood."

Piola was his Nuto, a tall slim boy. I had seen Cinto hobbling after him, along the Belbo.

"Who knows," I said, "why they make these fires?"

Cinto stood and listened. "In my time," I said, "the old people said they brought rain—Did your father make a bonfire? You would need rain this year. They're kindling the bonfires everywhere."

"It looks as if they're good for the land. They make it rich."

I seemed to have become someone else. I was speaking to him as Nuto had spoken to me.

"But how is it then that they always light it beyond the cultivated land?" I asked. "The next day you find the bed of the bonfire on the roads, beside the gullies, in the scrub . . ."

"You can't burn the vineyard anyway," he said, laughing.

"Yes, but you put manure on the cultivated land instead . . ."

We never finished these discussions, because an angry voice called him, or one of Piola's boys passed or a lad from Il Morone and Cinto would stop short and say, just as his father would have said, "Let's go and see what's happening," and went off.

I was never sure if he stayed beside me out of politeness or because he wanted to. It's true that when I used to tell him what the harbour at Genoa is like and how the cargoes are loaded and about the sound of the ships' sirens and the sailors covered with tattooing, he listened to me and his eyes narrowed. This boy, I thought, with that leg of his, will always starve in the country. He'll never be able to hoe or carry the big baskets. He won't even be able to do his military service and so he won't see the city. Unless I were to make him want to.

"This ship's siren," he said to me the day we were speaking about it, "is it like the siren they sounded at Canelli when the war was on?"

"Did you hear it?"

"I should think so. They say it was louder than the whistle of a train. They all heard it. At night they came out to see if they were bombing Canelli. I've heard it and I've seen the aeroplanes."

"But if you were still a baby in arms . . ."

"I swear that I remember."

When I told Nuto what I used to say to the boy, he pursed his lips as if to put the clarinet to his mouth and shook his head hard. "You're wrong," he said; "you're wrong. Why are you putting ideas into his head? As long as things don't change, he'll always have a bad time of it."

"Let him see what he's missing anyway."

"What do you want him to do about it? When he has seen that there are people in this world who are better off and worse off than himself, what good will it do him? If he is able to understand these things, all he has to do is to look at his father. All he has to do is to go into the piazza on Sunday, there's always someone begging, lame like himself, on the steps of the church. And inside, there are seats for the rich, with the name on them in brass."

"The more you open his eyes," I said, "the more he'll understand."

"But it's no use sending him to America. America is here already. We have our millionaires and people dying of hunger."

I said that Cinto would have to learn a trade and to do that he must get out of his father's clutches. "He would have been better to be born a bastard," I said. "He must get away and get out of the rut. Unless he mixes with people, he'll grow up like his father."

"There are lots of things want changing," said Nuto.

Then I told him that Cinto had his wits about him and what he needed was a farm which would be to him what La Mora had been for us. "La Mora was like the world," I said, "it was an America, a port. People came and went and worked and talked. Cinto is a boy now, but he will grow up. There will be girls. . . . Have you any idea what it means to mix with women who know a thing or two? With girls like Irene and Silvia?"

Nuto didn't say anything. I'd already noticed he didn't like to speak about La Mora. Although he had told me so much about his years in the band, he wouldn't go further back and talk about the time when we were boys. Or else he changed the subject to suit himself and began an argument. This time he said nothing and pursed his lips, and only when I told him about the bonfires in the stubble did he raise his head. "They're quite right to do it," he said. "They're awakening the earth."

"But Nuto," I said, "even Cinto doesn't believe that."

All the same, he said, he didn't know what it was, whether it was the heat or the blaze or something waking up inside the earth, anyhow in every field where they kindled a bonfire at the edge the crop grew quicker and heavier.

"This is something new," I said. "So you believe in the moon, too?"

"The moon—we must believe in the moon," said Nuto. "Try to cut down a pine tree when the moon is full and you will be eaten up by worms. You should wash a grape vat when the moon is new. As for grafting, unless you do it when the moon is only a few days old, it doesn't take."

Then I said I'd heard a few stories in my travels but these were the most far-fetched of the lot. There was no use having so much to say about the government and the priest's sermons, if he was going to believe in these superstitions like his great-great-grandmother. It was then that Nuto said very quietly that a superstition is a superstition only when it does harm to someone and if anyone were to use the moon and the bonfires to rob the peasants and keep them in the dark, then he would be the backward one and should be shot in the square. But before I could speak, I must become a countryman again.

An old man like Valino will know nothing else but he will know about the land.

We argued like mad dogs for a good while, but then he was called into the sawmill and I set off along the main road laughing. I had half a mind to go into La Mora, but it was hot. When I looked towards Canelli (it was a bright day and the sky was cloudless) I could see at one glance the plain of the Belbo with Gaminella in front and Salto to the side and the big house they call Il Nido, red in the middle of the plane trees, outlined against the slope of the furthest hill. So many vineyards and water-courses and burnt hillsides, almost white, made me want to be back in the vineyard at La Mora again, at the grape harvest, and see Sor Matteo's daughters coming with their basket. La Mora is behind the trees towards Canelli, below the slope where Il Nido stands.

Instead, I crossed the Belbo by the footbridge and while I walked along, I kept thinking that there was nothing more beautiful than a well-hoed, well-kept vineyard, with properly shaped leaves and that smell of the earth baked in the August sunshine. A well-worked vineyard is like a healthy body that lives and breathes and sweats. And when I looked round me again, I thought of these clumps of trees and reeds and these spinneys and watercourses—all names of villages and houses round about—which are quite useless and don't yield any harvest, yet nevertheless have their own beauty—each vineyard has its own patch of scrub—and give you pleasure when your eye lights on them and you know there are nests there. Women, I thought, have something of the same charm.

I'm a bit of a fool, I said. I've been away for twenty years and these villages were waiting for me. I remembered my disappointment the first time I walked the streets of Genoa—I walked in the middle of the road looking for a bit of grass. There was the harbour, certainly, and the girls' faces and the shops and the banks, but a clump of reeds, the smell of a bundle of brushwood, a patch of vineyard, where were they? And I knew the story of the moon and the bonfires after all, but I realised I'd forgotten I knew it.

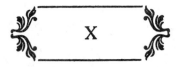

X

IF I BEGAN to think about these things, I was stopped, because so much came back to me, so many desires, so many old affronts, and I remembered the times I thought I had made a refuge for myself and had friends and a home where I could really put up my name and plant a garden. I thought I'd managed all this and had even got the length of saying to myself, "If I can make a little bit of money, I shall take a wife and send her and my son to the country. I want them to grow up there like me." But I have never had a son and don't let's speak about a wife—what use is this valley to a family that comes from across the sea and knows nothing about the moon and the bonfires? You must have grown up there and have it in your bones, like wine and polenta, and then you know it without needing to speak about it and everything you have carried about inside you for so many years without knowing awakens now at the rattle of the chain on a cart, at the swish of an ox's tail, at the taste of a bowl of minestra, at the sound of a voice heard in the square at night.

The fact of the matter was that Cinto—like me when I was a child—didn't know these things, and neither did anyone in the village unless perhaps someone who had been away. If I wanted to be understood by him or by anyone in the village, I must speak to them of the world outside and tell them my story—or better still don't tell them at all, but behave as if nothing had happened and carry about with me America and Genoa and the money I possessed stamped on my face and buttoned up in my pocket. People liked that sort of thing, except Nuto, of course, who was trying to understand me.

I used to meet people in the Albergo dell'Angelo, at the market, in the courtyards. Someone came to look for me, calling me once again the one from La Mora. They wanted to know what business I was transacting, if I was buying the Albergo dell'Angelo, if I was buying the bus. In the square they introduced me to the priest who spoke of a little ruined chapel, and to the clerk of the commune who drew me aside and said that my papers must still be in the town hall, if we wanted to look things up. I replied that I'd already been to the orphanage in Alessandria. The one who imposed least on my time was the Cavaliere, who knew all there was to know about the ancient history of the village and the misdeeds of the fascist mayor.

On the highroads and in the farms it was better, but they didn't believe me even there. Could I explain to anyone that what I sought was only to see something I had seen before? To see carts and haylofts, to see a wooden bucket, an iron gate, a chicory flower, a blue-checked scarf, a gourd to drink out of, the handle of a zappa. I liked the faces, too, the same as I'd always seen them; the old wrinkled women, the cautious oxen, the girls with flowers, the roofs of the dove-cotes. It seemed as if only seasons had passed since I saw them last, not years. The less difference there was from long ago in what I saw and heard—the droughts, the fairs, harvests they'd had before the world began—the better I liked them. And it was the same with minestra and wine-bottles and bill-hooks and tree trunks on the threshing-floor.

Here Nuto told me I was wrong and that I shouldn't put up with it, for on these hillsides people still live like beasts and not like human beings and the war hadn't done any good and everything was just like it had been before except for the dead.

We spoke about Valino and his sister-in-law, too. Whether Valino slept with her now was the least of it—what else could he do?—but there were terrible goings-on in that house. Nuto told me you could hear the women shrieking from the valley of the Belbo when Valino took off his belt and beat them like beasts and he thrashed Cinto, too—it wasn't the wine, they didn't have as much as that, it was the utter misery and his rage at his life which never gave him a break.

I had learnt, too, what had happened to Padrino and his family. Cola's daughter-in-law had told me, the same one who had wanted to sell me the house. At Cossano where they had gone with the little money they got from the sale of the croft, Padrino had died a few years ago, an old man chucked out on the road by his daughters' husbands. The younger one had married while still a girl and the other, Angiolina, a year afterwards, two brothers who lived at La Madonna delle Rovere in a farm above the woods. Up there they had lived with the old man and their children; they ate grapes and polenta and nothing else and they came down to bake their bread once a month, they were so out of the way. The two men worked hard and wore out their women and their oxen; the younger girl had died in a field, struck by lightning, and the other, Angiolina, had had seven children and then had taken to bed with a tumour in her side and had lain and moaned for three months—the doctor climbed up there once a year—and died without even seeing the priest. When his daughters were gone, there was no one else in the house to give the old man food and he had begun to go round the countryside and the fairs; Cola had a glimpse of him for the last time with a great white beard stuck with straw, the year before the war. He, too, had died in the end, on the threshing-floor of a farm, where he had gone to beg.

So it was no use to go to Cossano to look for my foster-sisters, to see if they still remembered me. I couldn't get out of my head the picture of Angiolina laid out with her mouth half-open like her mother that winter she died.

I went instead to Canelli one morning, along the railway line, by the road I'd gone so many times when I was at La Mora. I had to pass Salto and Il Nido, and I saw La Mora with the lime trees touching the roof, the terrace the girls used to sit on, the glass verandah and the low wing with the porch where we farm-hands used to live. I heard voices that I didn't know and held on my way.

I came into Canelli by a long avenue that wasn't there in my time but I noticed the smell at once—that sharp smell of wine lees, the breeze off the Belbo, and vermouth. The narrow streets were unchanged, with the flowers at the windows, the faces, the photographs and the big houses. There was more stir in the square —a new café, a petrol-filling station, the coming and going of motor-cycles in the dust. But the big plane tree was there. You could see there was still money about.

I spent the morning in the bank and the post office. Not a very big town, but who could tell how many other villas and big houses there were up there on the hills. So I had been quite right when I was a boy, the people of Canelli counted for something in the world and from here a window opened out on to it. From the bridge over the Belbo I looked at the valley and the low hills towards Nizza.

Nothing had changed, except that last year a boy had come on a cart to sell grapes with his father. Maybe for Cinto, too, Canelli would be a door into the world.

I noticed then that everything was changed. I liked

Canelli for its own sake, just as I liked the valley and the hills and the watercourses which opened out into it. I liked it because here everything finished, because it was the last village where season gave place to season, but not year to year. The manufacturers could make as much sparkling wine as they wanted, and set up offices, machines, waggon and store-houses—it was the same job as I was doing—and this was where the road began that passed through Genoa and might lead to anywhere. I had travelled along it from end to end, starting from Gaminella. If I had been a boy again, I should have gone along it once more. And what about it? Nuto, who had never really gone away, still wanted to understand the world and change it, and upset the cycle of the seasons. Or perhaps he didn't, and still believed only in the moon. But I, who didn't believe in the moon, knew that when all was said and done only the seasons matter and they are in your bones and they nurtured you when you were a boy. Canelli is the whole world—Canelli and the valley of the Belbo—and among the hills time stands still.

Towards evening I came back along the road beside the railway line. I passed the avenue, I passed beneath Il Nido, I passed La Mora. At the house on Salto, I found Nuto in overalls planing and whistling, with a scowl on his face. "What's the matter?"

Someone had been clearing a bit of rough ground and had found two other bodies on the slopes at Gaminella, two fascist spies with their heads bashed in and their shoes gone. The doctor and the police official had gone running up to identify them but what is there left to identify after two years? They must be *repubblichini* because the partisans died in the valley, shot in the squares, or hanged from the balconies or they were sent to Germany.

"What is there to be angry about?" I said. "That's an old story."

But Nuto kept turning these things over in his mind and scowled while he whistled.

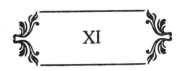

XI

A GOOD many years ago—here in Italy the war was on already—I had spent a night which comes back to my mind every time I walk along beside the railway line. I had a fair idea of what was going to happen—the war, internment, confiscation of enemy property—and I was trying to sell the shop and move over into Mexico. It was the nearest frontier and at Fresno I'd seen enough poor creatures from Mexico to know where I was going. Then the idea went out of my head because the Mexicans wouldn't have known what to make of my boxes of drink, and then the war came in earnest. I let it catch up with me—I was fed-up with looking ahead and running away from things and starting again the day after. I had to start all over again at Genoa last year.

The truth is that I knew it wouldn't last and the urge to do something, to work and take risks, melted away.

The life and the people I'd been used to for ten years now frightened and irritated me. Once again I drove my truck along the state highways and got as far as the desert, as far as Yuma, as far as the woods with the big trees. I had developed a yen to see something else besides the valley of San Joaquin and the faces I was used to. I knew that when the war was over I'd be driven to cross the sea, for the life I was leading was ugly and temporary.

Then I stopped pushing down the road to the south. It was too big a country—I should never get anywhere. I was no longer the lad who had got to California in eight months with the railway gangs. The more places you see, the less you belong to any of them.

That evening the truck broke down on me in the open country. I had planned to arrive at station 37 by nightfall and sleep there. It was cold, a dry cold full of dust, and the countryside was bare. Countryside is too good a word. As far as the eye could see there was an expanse of grey sand, full of thorns and little mounds that weren't hills, and the poles which marked the railway line. I tinkered about with the engine, but I couldn't do anything, for I'd no spare sparking plugs.

Then I began to get the wind up. All day I'd met only two cars and they were going to the coast. No one was going my way. I wasn't on the state highway, for I'd wanted to go across country. I said to myself "Wait. Someone will pass." No one passed until the next day. By good luck I had some blankets to wrap round me. "And what about tomorrow?" I said.

I had time to examine all the stones in the railway track, all the sleepers, the fluff from a withered thistle, the thick stems of two cactus plants in the hollow below the road. The stones in the track were burnt by the trains to that colour they have all over the world. A little wind screeched along the road, bringing a smell of salt. It was cold like winter. The sun was already down, the plain was disappearing.

I knew there were poisonous lizards and centipedes in holes in the plain, and here the serpent was supreme. The wild dogs began to howl. They weren't the danger I feared but they made me feel I was in the heart of America in a desert three hours by car from the nearest station. And night was coming on. The only sign of civilisation was the railway line and the rows of posts. If only the train would pass. Several times already I'd leant against a telegraph pole and listened to the humming of the wires, as boys do. The current came from the north and was going to the coast. I began to study the map again.

The dogs kept on howling in the grey sea that was the plain—a sound which cleft the air like a cock-crow—and made me feel cold and ill at ease. It was lucky I'd brought the bottle of whiskey with me. And I kept on smoking to calm my nerves. When it was dark, really dark, I lit the tail-light. I didn't dare to switch on the head-lights. If only a train would pass.

So many yarns came back to me, stories of people who had set out along these roads before they were made and had been found lying in a hollow, bones and clothes, nothing else. Bandits, thirst, loneliness, serpents. Here it was easy to understand that there had been a time when people drove themselves to death, when no one dismounted unless they meant to stay there for good. The thin line of the railway and the road was all the work they had put out on to it. Was it possible to leave the road and push on into the gullies among the cactus plants with the stars above you?

A dog sneezing, quite near, and the noise of falling stones made me jump. I put out the rear-light and lit it again almost at once. I remembered—and this made me less afraid—that towards evening, I'd overtaken a cartload of Mexicans drawn by a mule and loaded so that bundles protruded from all sides, sackloads of stuff, pots and pans and faces. It must be a family that was going to spend the season at San Bernardino or thereabouts. I had seen the children's thin little feet and the hooves of the mule trailing along the road. Their pants fluttered a dirty white and the mule stretched out its neck and pulled. When I passed them I'd thought that these wretched creatures would camp in some gully—they certainly wouldn't get to station 37 that night.

And where do these people have their home, I wondered. Is it possible to be born and live in a country like this? And yet they got used to it and went to look for seasonal work where it was to be found and led a life which gave them no peace, spending half the year in the mines and the other in the country. They hadn't needed to pass through the orphanage at Alessandria, the world had come to drive them from their home with hunger, or the railway, or their revolutions or their oil-wells, and now they were going hither and thither behind the mule. It was lucky they had a mule. There were some of them who set out barefoot without even a woman.

I got out of the cabin of the truck and stamped my feet on the road to warm them. The plain was as pale as death, blotched with vague shadows and in the darkness I could hardly see the road. The icy wind kept on screeching along the sand and now the dogs were silent; I heard whispers, the ghosts of voices. I had drunk enough not to be afraid of them any more. I smelt dry grass and a salty wind and I thought of the hills at Fresno.

Then came the train. It began by looking like a horse, a horse with its cart raised up on the rough stones and then I had glimpses of the light. For a moment I almost hoped it was a car or the cartload of Mexicans. Then its din filled the whole plain and it gave off showers of sparks. I wonder what the serpents and scorpions say about it. The train came almost on top of me standing on the road, lighting up with its windows the track, the cactus plants, a terrified animal that bounded away; and as it tore along banging from side to side, sucking in the air, I felt as if it were slapping me in the face. I had waited for it so long, but when darkness closed in again and the sand began to hiss round me, I said to myself that not even in a desert do these people leave you in peace. If I'd wanted to run away and hide tomorrow, so that I wouldn't be interned, I could feel already the hand of the policeman on my shoulder like the shock I got from the train. This was America.

I got back into the cabin, where I rolled myself up in a blanket and tried to doze as if I was at a street-corner at home. Then I thought to myself that for all the Californians' smartness, these ragged Mexicans were doing something that not one of them could have done—to camp out and sleep in the desert which they had made their home and where they even got along with the snakes. I'd better go to Mexico, I said. I bet it's the country for me.

Later in the night a loud barking woke me with a start. The whole plain was like a battlefield—or a farmyard. There was a reddish light and I jumped down, cramped and stiff with cold; a sliver of moon was piercing the low clouds and it looked like a gash from a knife and bathed the plain in a blood-red light. I stayed looking at it for a while. It terrified me.

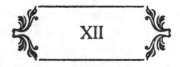

XII

NUTO WAS quite right. These two dead men from Gaminella caused no end of trouble. The doctor and the cashier and the three or four sporting young men who drank vermouth at the bar began to hold up their hands in horror and ask how many poor Italians who had only done their duty, had been barbarously assassinated by the reds. Because, they said under their breath, it's the reds who shoot people in the back of the neck without a trial. Then the schoolmistress passed, a little woman with glasses who was a sister of the secretary to the commune and owned vineyards of her own, and she began to shout that she was ready to go into the watercourses herself and find other bodies, all the bodies, and dig up any number of poor boys if it would get that communist scum, Valerio, or Pajetta, or the party official at Canelli put in prison or even hanged. Someone said, "It's difficult to accuse the communists. The partisans were autonomous here." "What does that matter?" said another. "Don't you remember the lame one with the scarf who requisitioned the blankets? And when they burnt the store. . . . Autonomous do you call them? There are all sorts. Do you remember the German?" "Whether they were autonomous or not," shrieked the

68

son of the Signora at the villa, "doesn't mean a thing. All the partisans were assassins."

"As far as I can see," said the doctor, looking at us closely, "you can't say that anyone in particular was to blame. It was a bloody business what with guerilla warfare and illegality. Probably these two were really spies. . . . But," he went on, raising his voice above the discussion that was beginning again, "who formed the first bands? Who wanted civil war? Who gave the Germans and the others such provocation? The communists. Always the communists. *They*'re responsible. *They*'re the assassins. It's an honour which we Italians grant them willingly. . . ."

His conclusion pleased everyone. Then I said I didn't agree with him. He asked me why. The year you spoke of, I said, I was still in America. (Silence.) And in America I was interned. (Silence.) In America, which is America after all, I said, the papers had carried a proclamation by the King and Badoglio which ordered all Italians to take to the hills, to engage in guerilla warfare, to attack the Germans and fascists in the rear. (Silence.) No one remembered about it now. They began to argue again.

I'd hardly left them when the schoolmistress cried out, "They're all bastards. It's our money they want, our land and our money, the same as in Russia. And they bump off anyone who protests."

Even Nuto came to the village to listen.

"Is it really true," I asked him, "that not one of these youngsters was a partisan and will say so? At Genoa the partisans even had a newspaper. . . ."

"No, none of them," said Nuto. "They're all people who put on the tricoloured scarf the day afterwards. Some of them were at Nizza, doing office work. The people who have really risked their skins don't want to talk about it."

It wasn't possible to identify the two bodies. They had taken them on a cart to the old hospital and a lot of people went to see them and came out screwing up their faces. "Ah well," said the women, standing at their doorways in the little streets, "we all come to it sooner or later. But that's a nasty end." Since neither of them had been tall and one of them had worn a medallion of S. Gennaro round his neck, the police official concluded they were from the south. He declared them "persons unknown" and closed the inquest.

It was the parish priest who didn't close it, but began poking his nose into things. He at once called together the mayor, the *carabiniere*, a committee of householders and the Sisters. The Cavaliere kept me informed for he bore the priest a grudge because he had taken away the brass plaque from the seat without telling him about it. "The seat where my mother used to kneel," he said. "My mother who did more good to the church than ten louts like him."

On the partisans the Cavaliere didn't pass any judgment. "Boys," he said, "boys who found themselves fighting a war. When I think that so many . . ."

In short, the priest was making capital out of it, for he hadn't got over the unveiling of the memorial to the partisans hanged in front of the Ca' Nere; it had been done without asking him, two years ago, by a socialist deputy come specially from Asti. At the meeting in the priest's house, he had got things off his chest. They'd all got it off their chest and agreed to act together. Since they couldn't denounce any of the former partisans, it was so long ago now, and there were no longer any "subversive elements" in the village, as the fascists would have called them, they made up their minds to work it up into a political issue which would reach the ears of the people in Alba, and have a fine service—solemn burial for the two victims, a public meeting and anathema of the reds. Watch and pray. Total mobilisation.

"I'm not one to rejoice at these times," said the Cavaliere. "War, as the French say, is a sale métier. But this priest is exploiting the dead, he'd exploit his mother, if he had one . . ."

I looked in at Nuto's to tell him the latest. He scratched his ear, looked at the ground and chewed his lips bitterly.

"I knew it," he said at last, "he tried a stunt like this with the gipsies."

"What gipsies?"

He told me that in 1945 a band of young lads had captured two gipsies who for months had been coming and going, double-crossing and indicating the partisans' dispositions. "You know how it is—there were all kinds in the bands. People from all over Italy and from abroad. And people who didn't know what it was all about. You never saw such a mess. Well, instead of taking them to headquarters they take them and put them down a well and make them tell how often they'd been to the militia barracks. Then they tell one of them, who had a fine voice, to sing for his life. And he sings, sitting on top of the well, tied hand and foot, he sings like mad and puts all he has into it. While he's singing they take a mattock to them and lay them both out. We dug them up two years ago and immediately the priest preached a sermon about them in church. He has never preached sermons about the people at the Ca' Nere, as far as I know."

"If I were you," I said to him, "I'd go and ask him to say a mass for the ones who were hanged. If he refuses his name will be mud."

Nuto grinned mirthlessly. "He's the kind of man who might do it and hold his protest meeting just the same."

And so on Sunday the funeral took place. The municipal authorities were there, the *carabinieri*, the veiled women, the daughters of Mary. That devil had got the Flagellants, too, in yellow cassocks, it was hell. Flowers all over the place. The schoolmistress, who owned some vineyards, had sent round the little girls to ransack the gardens. The priest in his best vestments and shining spectacles preached the sermon on the church steps. He preached big stuff. He said the times had become diabolical and souls were in danger. That too much blood had been spilt and too many young people were still listening to words of hate. That the country, the family, and religion were still threatened. Red, the fair colour of the martyrs, had become the badge of Antichrist and in his name so many crimes had been and were being committed. We, too, must repent and purify ourselves and make atonement—giving Christian burial to the two unknown young men barbarously slaughtered, sent home, God knows, without the consolation of the sacraments—make atonement and pray for them and raise a barrier of faithful hearts. He even said a few words in Latin. We must bear witness before the men of violence, those who have no fatherland and no God. And let them not think that the enemy is defeated. In too many Italian communes, he still flourishes his red flag.

I must say I didn't mind the sermon. It was a very long time since I had heard a priest say his say on the steps of the church in the hot sunshine. And to think that when I was a boy and Virgilia took us to mass, I thought that the voice of the priest was a thing like thunder or the sky or the seasons, which helped the fields and the harvests, for the salvation of the living and the dead. Now I noticed that the dead helped *him*. We really shouldn't grow old or get to know the world.

It was Nuto who didn't appreciate the sermon. In the piazza one of his friends winked and muttered to him in passing. And Nuto kept fidgeting miserably. He couldn't do anything else because they were dead and it didn't matter whether they were blackshirts or had died decently. When they're dealing with the dead, priests are always right. I knew it and so did he.

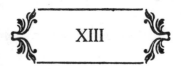

XIII

THEY KEPT going over this story in the village. The priest was in fine fettle. He struck the iron while it was hot the next day again and said a mass for the dead, for the living who were still in danger, for those who were yet to be born. He advised them not to enrol in subversive parties, not to read anti-Christian and obscene papers, not to go to Canelli except on business and not to stop at the inn, and he told the girls to let down their dresses. If you had heard the gossiping women and the shop-keepers talking in the village, you'd think blood had flowed like a grape-juice in the vine presses. Everyone had been robbed and burnt out, and all the women got with child. Until the former fascist mayor said plainly, sitting at one of the tables in the Albergo dell'Angelo, that this sort of thing didn't happen before. Then the lorry-driver, a hard-faced man from Calosso, leapt to his feet and asked him where the sulphur for the co-operative had got to before.

I went back to Nuto's and found him measuring axles, and still in a bad temper. In the house his wife was suckling the baby. She cried to him from the window that he was a fool to take it seriously and politics had never made anyone better off yet. All the way along the road from the village to Salto, I'd been turning things over in

74

my mind but I couldn't put them into words. Now Nuto looked at me and flung down the rule and asked me harshly if I hadn't had enough yet of whatever it was I liked about these wretched villages.

"You should have done it when you got the chance," I said to him. "Any fool knows how to seal up a wasp's nest."

Then he shouted in at the window "Comina, I'm going out." He picked up his jacket and said "Come and have a drink." While I waited for him, he gave some orders to the apprentices in the shed and then he turned to me and said:

"I'm fed-up. Let's get out of it."

We climbed up by Salto. At first we didn't speak or only said, "The grapes are good this year." We passed between the watercourse and Nuto's vineyard. We left the narrow road and took the path which was so steep we had to go sideways. At the corner of a row of vines, we ran into Berta, who never left his own bit of ground now. I stopped a minute to pass the time of day and make myself known—I'd never thought to find him still alive and so toothless—but Nuto kept straight on and only said "Good day." Berta certainly didn't know me.

I had climbed once before as far as here where the farmyard of Lo Spirito ended. We used to come up here in November to steal the medlars. I began to look down at the dried-up vineyards, the overhanging terraces, the reddish top of Salto, the Belbo and the woods. Even Nuto slowed down now, and we went on doggedly, holding on to each other.

"The damnable thing," said Nuto, "is that we are all

so stupid. The priest has the whole place under his thumb."

"What do you mean? Why don't you answer him back?"

"You mean I should answer him back in church? This is a place where you can only make speeches in church, otherwise they don't believe you. The obscene and anti-Christian press, he says—as if they could even read the almanac!"

"You must get out of the village," I said, "and try a change of air. It's different at Canelli. You heard even him say that Canelli is hell itself."

"Isn't that enough?"

"It's a beginning, anyway. Canelli is the road to the outside world. After Canelli comes Nizza. After Nizza, Alessandria. You'll never do anything alone."

Nuto heaved a sigh and stood still. I stopped for a minute, too, and looked down into the valley.

"If you want to do anything," I said, "you must have contacts with the world outside. Haven't you political parties who work for you, deputies, men for this very job? Speak out and get to know each other. That's what they do in America. The strength of the parties is made up of a whole lot of little places like this. The priests don't work alone, they've a whole body of other priests behind them. Why doesn't that deputy who spoke at Ca' Nere come back?"

We sat down in the shade of a clump of reeds on the hard grass and Nuto told me why the deputy didn't come back. From the day of the liberation—that longed-for 25th April—everything had gone from bad to worse. In these days something had been achieved at least. If the *mezzadri* and the poor of the village didn't go about the world themselves, the world had come, in the war years, to awaken *them*. There had been men from all parts, from the south, from Tuscany, townsfolk, students, evacuees, workers—even the Germans and the fascists had done some good, they had opened people's eyes, even the stupidest, and made people show themselves in their true colours, one on one side, one on the other— this man wanted to exploit the peasants and I wanted to share the future with them. And the men who had refused their military service and the deserters had shown the government that it isn't enough just to want to get mixed up in a war. Of course, with all that confusion, some things were done which shouldn't have been done —people robbed and murdered without any motive, but not many certainly—"Not nearly as many," said Nuto, "as the people who had the upper hand in the old days had put out on the street or worked to death. And what happened then?" he asked. They had left off being on their guard, they had believed in the Allies, in the people who had had the upper hand before, people who now, when the storm was past, crept out from the cellars, from the big houses and the priests' houses and the convents. And now we've reached the point, said Nuto, where a priest who owes it to the partisans if he can still peal his bells—they saved them for him—defends the fascist republic and two of its spies. And even if they were shot for no reason at all, he said, was it his place to insult the partisans who died like flies to save their country?

While he was speaking, I saw Gaminella opposite, it looked bigger than ever at this height, a hill like a planet, and from here I could see flat slopes and little trees and paths that I had never seen before. One day, I thought to myself, I must climb up there. It's a bit of the world, too. I asked Nuto "Were there any partisans up there?"

"The partisans were everywhere," he said. They hunted them down like wild beasts. They died everywhere. One day I would hear shots at the bridge and the next day they were beyond the Bormida. And they never closed an eye in peace and no hide-out was safe. There were spies everywhere."

"Were you a partisan? Were you there?"

Nuto swallowed hard and shook his head. "Everyone did something—it wasn't enough, but there was always the danger that a spy would send them to burn down your house."

I gazed from up there at the plain of the Belbo and the lime trees and the farmyard at La Mora—all the fields looked small and unfamiliar. I'd never seen it from above, it looked so tiny.

"I passed La Mora the other day," I said. "The pine tree isn't at the gate any more."

"Nicoletto, the accountant, made them cut it down. The fool! He made them cut it down because all the beggars used to stop in the shade and beg. Do you see? He's got through half the estate and he still isn't happy. He doesn't even like a poor man to stop in the shade and ask him how he did it."

"But how has everything gone to the devil like this?

People who kept a carriage. With the old man it wouldn't have happened."

Nuto didn't answer and tore up tufts of dry grass.

"Nicoletto wasn't the only one of the family," I said. "What about the girls? When I think of them, my heart misses a beat. All right, they both liked to have a good time and Silvia was a fool who went to bed with anyone, but as long as the old man was alive, they always managed to keep her in order. It's funny the stepmother should have died. And the little girl, Santina, how did she finish up?"

Nuto was still thinking about his priest and the spies because he made a wry mouth again and swallowed hard.

"She stayed at Canelli," he said. "She couldn't get on with Nicoletto. She gave the blackshirts a good time. Everybody knows about it. Then one day she disappeared."

"Is that so?" I asked. "But what's happened to her? Our good little girl? To think that she was so pretty when she was six."

"You didn't see her at twenty," said Nuto. "The other two were nothing compared to her. They spoilt her; Sor Matteo had no eyes for anyone but her. Do you remember when Irene and Silvia wouldn't go out with their stepmother so that they wouldn't look plain beside her? Well, Santa was more beautiful than the two of them and her mother put together."

"So she disappeared? And they don't know what's happened to her?"

"They know." Nuto said. "The little bitch!"

"What's so bad about that?"

"She was a bitch and a spy."

"Did they kill her?"

"Let's go home," said Nuto. "I wanted to enjoy myself but I can't, even with you."

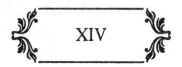

XIV

WE SEEMED to be fated. I often wondered why there was no one left now but Nuto and me, just the two of us, out of so many people once alive. Once upon a time I'd had a longing within me (one morning in a bar in San Diego I nearly went mad with it) to come out on to the main road, to push open the iron gate between the pine and the lime trees at the corner, to hear the voices and the laughter and the hens and say, "Here I am, I've come back," watching their bewildered faces—the farm-hands, the women, the dog, the old man—and the grey eyes and the brown eyes of the girls would have recognised me from the terrace—it was a longing I'd never get rid of now. I had come back. I had come out on to the road, I had made my fortune—I slept at the Albergo dell'Angelo and talked with the Cavaliere—but the faces, the voices, and the hands which should have touched me and recognised me, were gone. They had been gone for a while. What was left behind was like a piazza the day after the fair, or a vineyard after the grape harvest or going back to eat alone after someone has let you down. Nuto, the only one left, was changed, he had become a man like myself. To make a long story short, I was a man, too. I was someone else—if I had indeed found La Mora as I had known it the first winter, and the summer after, and then summer following winter again, day and night through all these years, I certainly wouldn't have known what to do with myself. Maybe I came from too far away—I didn't belong to this house any more, I wasn't like Cinto now, the world had changed me.

On these summer evenings, when we sat late under the pine tree or on the beam in the courtyard—passers-by stopped for a while at the gate, women laughed and someone came out from the stable—the talk always finished when the old men, and Lanzone, the grieve, and Serafina, and sometimes, if he came down, Sor Matteo, said, "Yes, yes, boys and girls, try to grow up, that's what our grandfathers used to say—you'll see what it's like when it's your turn." At that time I didn't understand what this growing-up meant, I thought it was only being able to do difficult things, like buying a pair of oxen, or calculating the price of grapes, or using the threshing machine. I didn't know that growing-up meant to go away, to get old, to see people die, to come back and find La Mora as it was now. I thought to myself, I'll eat my hat if I don't win the flag at the races, if I don't buy myself a farm, if I don't get on better than Nuto. And I thought about the gig which belonged to Sor Matteo and the girls, and about the terrace, and the piano in the drawing-room, and the wine-buckets and the granaries and the fair at San Rocco. I was a boy who was growing up.

The year the hailstorm came and Padrino had to sell the croft and go as a farm-hand to Cossano, he had sent me several times to do a day's work at La Mora. I was only thirteen, but I was doing something to help and I was bringing home a few pence. I used to cross the Belbo in the morning—once Giulia came too—and along with the women and the farm-hands and Cerino and Serafina, I helped to gather walnuts or cut millet or pick the grapes or look after the animals. I liked the big farmyard—so many people could get into it and no one looked for you—and then it was near the main road, beneath Salto. So many new faces there were, and the carriage and the horse and the windows with the curtains. For the first time I saw flowers, real flowers, like those in church. Under the lime-trees, beside the gate, was the garden, full of zinnias and lilies and dahlias—I realised that you can grow flowers like fruit—they produced flowers instead of fruit and when they were gathered they were for the use of the Signora and her daughters, who went out for them with their parasols and arranged them in vases when they were in the house. Irene and Silvia were eighteen or twenty then, I saw them sometimes. Then there was Santina, their half-sister, who was newly born, and whom Emilia ran up to rock every time she heard her cry.

In the evening at the croft at Gaminella I told all this to Angiolina and Padrino and Giulia (if she hadn't come, too), and Padrino used to say, "There's a man who could buy us all up. Lanzone's got a fine job with him. Sor Matteo will never die at the roadside, that's certain." Even the hail which had stripped our vineyard hadn't fallen beyond the Belbo and all the farms on the plain and up on Salto shone like the flanks of a bullock.

"We're finished," said Padrino. "How am I going to pay the mortgage?" He was getting on and his great fear was to die without a roof to his head or a bit of land.

"Let's sell it then," said Angiolina, through her clenched teeth. "We'll get in somewhere."

"If only your mother was still here," muttered Padrino.

I realised that this autumn would be the last and when I went through the vineyard or up the gully, I always held my breath in case they would call me or someone would come to send me away. Because I knew I wasn't anybody at all.

Then the priest came into it—the one that was the priest then, old and big-made with hard knuckles—and bought it for someone else; he spoke with the co-operative and went himself as far as Cossano to arrange about the girls and Padrino, and when the cart came to take the cupboard and the mattresses, I went into the stable to untie the goat. It wasn't there any more, they had sold it, too. While I was crying about the goat, the priest arrived—he had a big grey umbrella and muddy shoes—and scowled at me. Padrino went off round the farmyard, pulling at his moustache. "Don't you be a baby," the priest said. "What is this house to you? You're young and you've got a lot of time in front of you. Try to grow up and repay these people for what they've done for you."

I knew everything by this time. I knew it, and I was crying. The girls were in the house and they didn't come out because the priest was there. "At the farm where Padrino's going," he said, "there's hardly room even for your sisters. We've found you a good place. They'll make you work there."

And so, when the days began to get colder, I started work at La Mora. When I crossed the Belbo for the last time, I didn't look back. I crossed it with my clogs and my bundle slung over my shoulder and four mushrooms in a handkerchief that Angiolina was sending to Serafina. Giulia and I had found them in Gaminella.

Cirino, the farm-hand, met me at La Mora—he'd got permission from the grieve and Serafina. Without losing any time he showed me the stable where the cow and the oxen were and, behind a partition, the horse for the gig. Against the wall there was a pile of trappings and whips with little bows of ribbon. He said I would sleep in the hayloft that night and then he would put a palliasse in the granary for me where he slept himself. This and the big room with the wine-press and the kitchen had cement instead of beaten earth for a floor. In the kitchen was a cupboard with glass doors full of cups, and above the mantelpiece hung festoons of shiny red paper which Emilia dared me to touch. Serafina kept my stuff and asked me if I meant to grow any more; she said to Emilia that she'd find me a jacket for the winter. The first work I did was to break up a sheaf of brushwood and grind the coffee.

It was Emilia who told me I was like an eel. That evening we ate after it was dark, by the light of a petrol lamp, all together in the kitchen—the two women, Cirino, and Lanzone, the grieve, who said it was all right to hold back at table but work should be done with a will. He asked me about Virgilia and Angiolina and Cossano. Then they called Emilia upstairs, the grieve went out into the stable and I was alone with Cirino at the table laden with bread and cheese and wine. Then I plucked up courage and Cirino told me there was enough for everyone at La Mora.

And so winter came on and a lot of snow fell and the Belbo froze over, but we were warm in the kitchen or in the stable, and we had only to shovel the snow in the farmyard and in front of the gate or go for another bundle of wood, or I would put the withies in to soak for Cirino, or go for water, or play at marbles with the other boys. Christmas came, the New Year, Epiphany; we roasted the chestnuts and drew the wine and we ate turkey twice and goose once. Sor Matteo and his daughters and the Signora had the gig harnessed to go to Canelli; once they brought home almond cake and gave some to Emilia. On Sundays I went to mass in the village with the boys from Salto and the women, and carried the bread to be baked. The hill at Gaminella was bare and white with snow—I used to see it through the dry branches beside the Belbo.

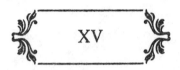

XV

I DON'T know if I'll buy a bit of land or if I'll court Cola's daughter—I don't think so, my day is all telephone calls now, and business errands and city pavements—but even before I came back, when I was coming out of a bar or jumping on to a train, or coming home in the evening, I used to know what season it was from the smell of the air and remembered it was the time to prune, or mow, to put on the copper-sulphate or wash the vats or strip the reeds.

At Gaminella I was nothing, at La Mora I learnt a trade. Here no one spoke to me any more about the five lire from the town hall and by the next year I never gave Cossano a thought—I was Anguilla and I was earning my keep. At first it wasn't easy because the farm of La Mora stretched from the plain of the Belbo half-way up the hill, and after the vineyard at Gaminella which Padrino could work himself, I used to get mixed up with so many animals and so many different crops and so many new faces. I had never seen work done by farm-hands before or so many carts loaded with grain and millet or so big a grape harvest. In the fields below the road alone we counted the beans and lentils by the sackful. Between ourselves and the family there were ten mouths to feed and we sold the grapes and the grain and the walnuts, we sold everything and the grieve still had some to put aside. Sor Matteo kept his horse, his daughters played the piano and were always going to the dressmakers at Canelli and Emilia waited on them at table.

Cirino taught me how to look after the oxen and change the litter when they'd hardly fouled it. Lanzone wants the oxen kept like brides, he said. He taught me to groom them and prepare their draught and give them a forkful of hay, neither too much nor too little. At the feast of San Rocco they took them to the fair, and the grieve really earned his pay with them. In spring when we spread the manure it was I who led the smoking cart. When the fine weather came we had to get out in the fields before daybreak and yoke the ox in the farmyard in the dark, under the stars. Now I had a jacket which reached to my knees and I was warm. At sunrise Serafina and Emilia came with the watered wine, or I ran to the house and we ate our breakfast and the grieve gave out the day's work; they began to stir upstairs, people passed by on the road, at eight you heard the whistle of the first train. I spent the day cutting green stuff for fodder, turning the hay, drawing water, preparing the copper-sulphate and watering the kitchen-garden. On the days when the hired men were there, the grieve sent me to keep an eye on them to see that they hoed properly and sprayed well under the vine-leaves and that they didn't stop to talk at the bottom of the vineyard. And the hired men told me that I was one of them and ought to let them smoke their fag-ends in peace.

"Watch how to do it," Cirino used to say spitting on

his hands and lifting the heavy hoe. "Another year and you'll have to put your back into it, too."

Because I didn't really work yet, the women called me into the courtyard, sent me to do this or that, kept me in the kitchen while they made the *pasta* and lit the stove, and I stayed and listened and saw who came and went. Cirino, who was a farm-hand like me, remembered that I was only a boy and gave me jobs to do that kept me under the eyes of the women. He didn't have much to do with the women himself, he was getting on, with no family, and on Sunday when he lit his cigar he told me he didn't even like to go to the village, but would rather listen from behind the gate to the talk of the passers-by. Sometimes I hurried away along the main road as far as the house at Salto and the shop that belonged to Nuto's father. The shavings and the geraniums that are still there now were there then. Whoever passed by, whether going to Canelli or coming back from it, stopped to pass the time of day and the joiner worked away with his plane and his chisel and his saw and talked to everyone about Canelli, about long ago, about politics and music and madmen, about the world. Some days I had errands to go and so I could stop to listen, and I drank in every word they were saying while I played with the other boys, as if the grown-ups were talking specially for my benefit. Nuto's father read the paper.

Even in Nuto's house Sor Matteo was well spoken of; they spoke about the time when he was a soldier in Africa and had been given up for dead by everyone, by the priest and his betrothed and his mother, and how the dog howled night and day in the courtyard. And one evening the train from Canelli passed behind the trees and the dog began to bark frantically and his mother knew at once that up there Sor Matteo was coming back on it. Old stories these—at that time La Mora was only an ordinary farmhouse, the girls weren't born yet, and Sor Matteo was always at Canelli, always going the rounds in his gig, always hunting. He was wild, but within limits. He managed his affairs and laughed and ate the while. Even yet in the mornings he ate a red pepper and drank good wine on top of it. He had buried a while back the wife who had borne him his two daughters; shortly afterwards he had another daughter by the woman who had come to live with him and for all that he was old now, it was always he who joked and gave orders.

Sor Matteo had never worked on the land—he was a gentleman, was Sor Matteo, but he hadn't studied or travelled either. Except for that time in Africa, he had never been further than Acqui. He had been mad about women—even Cirino said so—as his father and his grandfather had been set on gathering gear and had added one farm to another. It ran in their blood, compounded of the soil and vigorous desires, and they liked to have abundance, whether of wine and grain and meat, or women and money. While his grandfather had been one to hoe and tend his own land, his sons had changed and preferred to enjoy themselves. But even now Sor Matteo could tell at a glance how many thousand litres a vineyard should produce, how many sacks that field should yield, how much manure that meadow needed. When the grieve took him the accounts, they shut themselves in a room upstairs, and Emilia, who used to take them coffee, would tell us that Sor Matteo knew the accounts by heart and remembered about a barrow or a basket or a day lost the year before.

For a while I never went up the flight of steps that led upstairs behind the glass door—they made me too frightened. Emilia, who came and went and could order me about because she was the grieve's niece, and who waited at table in her apron when they had visitors upstairs—Emilia sometimes called me from the window or the terrace to come up, to do this or that, or bring something to her. I tried to hide in the porch. Once when I had to carry up a pail, I put it down on the landing and fled. And I remember the morning when the gutter above the terrace had to be repaired and they called me to hold the ladder for the man who was sorting it. I crossed the landing and went through two dark rooms full of furniture and almanacs and flowers—it was all polished and shining like mirrors—I was walking on the red tiles, barefoot, when out came the Signora in black with a medallion round her neck and a sheet over her arm, and looked at my feet. From the terrace Emilia shouted, "Anguilla, come along, Anguilla."

"Emilia is calling me," I stammered.

"Go along then," she said. "Be quick!"

They were spreading out the newly washed sheets on the terrace and the sun was shining and I could see in the background, towards Canelli, the big house they called Il Nido. Fair-haired Irene was there, too, leaning on the railing with a towel round her shoulders, for she was drying her hair. And Emilia, who was holding the ladder herself, shouted, "Come over here. Get a move on."

Irene said something and they all laughed. All the time I held the ladder, I kept looking at the wall and the cement, and to relieve my feelings, I thought of what we boys talked about when we went to hide among the reeds.

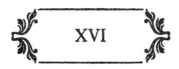

XVI

FROM La Mora you can get down to the Belbo more easily than from Gaminella because the road from Gaminella overhangs the water among briars and acacias, while the bank here is all sand and willows and short reeds like grass and scattered clumps of trees that stretch as far as the cultivated fields of La Mora. Sometimes in the hot weather when Cirino sent me to prune or gather willow branches, I used to tell my chums and we would meet on the river bank—one came with a broken basket and another with a sack, and we took off our clothes and fished and played. We ran about in the sun on the hot sand. It was here I boasted of my nickname of Anguilla —the Eel—and Nicoletto said he would tell on us because he was jealous and began to call me bastard. Nicoletto was the son of an aunt of the Signora's and stayed at Alba in the winter time. We began to fling stones at each other and I had to watch not to hurt him so that he wouldn't have any bruises to show at La Mora in the evening. Then there were the times that the grieve or the women working in the fields saw us, and then naked as I was I had to run and hide and come through into the fields pulling on my trousers. A punch on the head and a sharp word from the grieve were things that no one could take away from me afterwards.

But all this was nothing compared with the life that Cinto led now. His father was always after him and kept an eye on him from the vineyard, and the two women used to call him and curse him and, instead of stopping at Piola's, they wanted him to come home with the green fodder or the heads of millet or the ox dung or the rabbit skins. There wasn't enough of anything in that house. There was no bread. They drank wine lees and ate polenta and lentils, not many lentils. I know all about it, I know what it feels like to hoe or spray the vines with sulphate in the heat of the day and be hungry and thirsty the while. I know that the vineyard at the croft wasn't enough for us and we didn't have to share it with anyone.

Valino didn't speak to anyone. He hoed and pruned and tied and spat and kept things in repair; he gave the ox a kick in the face and chewed polenta and looked at the farmyard and gave orders with his eyes. The women ran to do his bidding, Cinto made off. Then in the evening when it was time to go to bed—Cinto nibbled his supper in the watercourse—Valino got a hold of him, he got a hold of the women, he got a hold of whoever he could lay hands on, at the door, or on the ladder leading to the hayloft, and thrashed them with his belt.

The little I'd heard from Nuto was enough for me and

Cinto's face, too, when I used to meet him on the road and speak to him, always on edge, and wondering what they were doing at Gaminella now. There was the story of the dog whom they kept tied up without food and at night it smelt the hedgehogs and the bats and the weasels and leapt like a mad thing to catch them, and bayed, and bayed at the moon that looked like polenta. Then Valino got out of bed and half-killed him, too, with blows and kicks.

One day I persuaded Nuto to come to Gaminella to look at the vat. He didn't want to have anything to do with it.

"I know," he said, "that if I speak to him I'll miscall him, and tell him he's living like a wild animal. How can I say that? Would it be any use? First of all the government would have to do away with money and the people who defend it."

Going along the road I asked him if he was convinced it was really poverty that brutalised men. "Have you never read in the papers about these millionaires who take drugs and shoot themselves? There are vices that cost money. . . ."

He answered that there you were—it's the money that does it, always the money, whether you had it or not, as long as it existed there was no way out for anyone.

When we got to the croft, the sister-in-law, Rosina, came out—the one who had whiskers, too—and said Valino was at the well. This time he didn't keep us waiting; he came and said to the woman, "Take a stick to that dog," and we hadn't been in the farmyard a moment when he said to Nuto, "You want to see the vat, then?"

I knew where the vat was, I knew the low-roofed cellar with the broken tiles and the cobwebs. I said, "I'll wait for you in the house," and at last I put my foot on the ladder.

I hadn't even time to look round inside when I heard someone whimpering and groaning softly and calling as if her throat was too tired to raise her voice. Outside the dog was struggling and howling. I heard whines and a dull blow and sharp cries—they'd given it to him.

By this time I could see. The old woman was sitting on a mattress against the wall; she was huddled in the corner, half-dressed, with her dirty feet sticking out, and she looked round the room and she looked at the door and kept on moaning and crying. The mattress was burst and the stuffing was coming out.

The old woman was tiny with a face as big as your fist, like those babies that gurgle with closed fists while the mother sings softly over the cradle. The room was stuffy and smelt of stale urine and vinegar. I realised that she went on like this night and day and she didn't even know she was doing it. With staring eyes she watched us at the door without changing her tone and without speaking to us.

I heard Rosina behind and I stepped forward. I tried to catch her eye and I was going to say, "She's dying, what's wrong with her?" But the sister-in-law didn't reply to my gesture; she said instead, "Would you please to sit down?" and lifting a wooden chair, she put it in front of me.

The old woman kept moaning like a sparrow with a broken wing. I looked round the room which was so small and changed. Only the little window was the same and the flies that flew about and the crack in the stone above the chimney. Above a box against the wall there was a pumpkin now and two glasses and a bunch of garlic.

I came out almost immediately with the sister-in-law behind me, like a dog. Under the fig tree I asked what was wrong with the old woman. She answered that she was old and spoke to herself and told her beads.

"Is that so? Doesn't she complain of pain?"

"At her age," said the woman, "it's all pain. All they can do is complain." She looked askance at me. "We women all come to that," she said.

Then she went to the edge of the field and began to yell, "Cinto, Cinto" as if they were cutting her throat, and she was weeping into the bargain. Cinto didn't come.

Instead Nuto and the father came out of the stable. "You've a fine beast there," Nuto was saying. "Do you get enough food for it here?"

"You're crazy," said Valino. "That's the *padrona's* affair."

"Things have come to a pretty pass," said Nuto, "when an owner provides food for the beast, but not for the men who till the soil!"

Valino was waiting. "Let's go quickly for any sake," said Nuto. "I'll send you the putty, then."

While we were going down the path he muttered that there were some people who would have taken a glass of wine from Valino. "And just look at the life he has," he said furiously.

Then we fell silent. I was thinking about the old woman. Cinto came out from behind the reeds with a

95

bundle of green stuff for fodder. He hobbled along quickly to meet us and Nuto said I'd courage to put ideas into his head.

"What ideas? Any other life would be better for him."

Every time I met Cinto I thought of giving him a few lire but then I held back. He wouldn't have been able to enjoy them, for what could he do with them? But this time we stopped and it was Nuto who said:

"Did you find the adder?"

Cinto made a face and said: "If I find it, I'll cut off its head."

"If you don't annoy it, the adder won't bite you," said Nuto.

Then I remembered when I was a boy myself and I said to Cinto: "If you're passing the Albergo dell'Angelo on Sunday, I'll give you a fine clasp-knife."

"Will you?" said Cinto, his eyes opening wide.

"I said I would. Do you ever go to Nuto's house at Salto? You'd like it. There are benches and planes and screwdrivers. If your father would let you, I'd have you taught a trade."

Cinto shrugged his shoulders. "My father . . ." he muttered. "I won't tell him."

When he'd gone, Nuto said, "I understand everything, but not a boy who comes into the world crippled like that. What's he going to do there?"

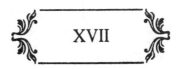

XVII

Nuto says he can remember the first time he saw me at La Mora. They were killing the pig and the women had all run away except Santina who was just learning to walk then and arrived at the very moment when the pig was spouting blood.

"Take that child away," the grieve had shouted and Nuto and I had run after her and caught her, getting not a few kicks for our pains. But if Santina was on her feet and running about it meant I had been a year at La Mora by then and we had seen each other before. I think the first time was before I went to La Mora at all—the autumn before the great hail-storm, when we were stripping the millet. We were in the farmyard at night, a crowd of us, farm-hands, boys, peasants from round about and women—and they sang and laughed, sitting on the long heaps of millet, and we stripped it amid the dry dusty smell of the withered leaves and threw the yellow heads against the wall of the porch. And Nuto was there that night and when Cirino and Serafino went round with the wine, he drank his like a man. He must have been fifteen but to me he seemed a man already. Everyone was speaking and telling stories and the lads were making the girls laugh. Nuto had brought his guitar and he played on it instead of stripping the millet. He could play well even at that time. At the end they all danced and shouted: "Well done, Nuto!"

But that night came round every year and perhaps Nuto is right when he says we had seen each other some other time. He was already working with his father in the house at Salto; I used to see him working at the bench but he didn't wear overalls. And he didn't stay long at the bench. He was always inclined to break loose and I knew that if I went with him we wouldn't simply play boys' games or waste our time—something always happened, we talked about things or we met someone or we found a special nest, an animal we hadn't seen before, or else we got to a new place; in short it was always something gained, something to talk about. And then I liked Nuto because we got on together and he treated me like a friend. Even then he had those piercing cat's eyes of his and when he had said something, finished up by saying: "If I'm wrong, put me right." And so I began to understand that you didn't speak for the sake of speaking, to say that you had done this or that, what you had eaten or drunk, but to work out an idea, to find out what makes the world go round. I had never thought about it before. But Nuto knew a lot about it—he was like a grown man; some summer evenings he came to sit late under the pine-tree (on the terrace there were Irene and Silvia and their mother) and he joked with them all and carried on at great length, telling stories about farms, about men with their wits about them and men who hadn't, about people who played in the band and contracts haggled out with the priest so that he seemed to be his father over again. Sor Matteo said to him: "I'd like to see how you get on when you're called up. They'll knock some of the nonsense out of you in the regiment." And Nuto replied: "They'll have a job to knock it all out."

To listen to this talk, to be Nuto's friend and know him so well had the same effect on me as drinking wine or listening to music. I was ashamed to be only a boy, a farm-hand, and not know how to chatter away like him, and I thought I'd never manage to do anything on my own. But he gave me confidence and told me he would teach me to play the cornet and take me to the fair at Canelli and make me have ten shots at the target in the shooting-booth. He told me that it isn't what you do but how you do it that shows whether you are clever or not and that some mornings when he wakened he felt like going to the bench himself and setting about making a table. "What are you frightened at?" he said. "You learn a thing by doing it. If you want to do it, that's enough. If I'm wrong, put me right."

In the years that followed I learned a great deal more from Nuto—or perhaps it was only that I was growing up and beginning to understand things on my own. But it was he who explained to me why Nicoletto was so nasty. "He doesn't know any better," he said. "He thinks that because he stays in Alba and wears shoes every day and no one makes him work, he's a cut above us peasants. And his people send him to school. It's you who keep him by working his family's land. But he doesn't even see that." It was Nuto who told me that you can go anywhere by train and that where the railway line ends the ports begin and the ships have their own time-table and the whole world is a network of roads and ports, a continual coming and going of people and some build and some undo what has been built, and everywhere there are people who can do things and others who can't. He told me the names of a lot of countries, too, and said that if you wanted to know all about them you only had to read the newspapers. And so some days when I was in the fields or in the vineyards above the road, hoeing away in the sun, and heard through the peach trees the train arriving and filling the valley with its noise as it came or went from Canelli—at these times I stopped and leant on my hoe and watched the smoke and the carriages and looked at Gaminella and the fine house they called Il Nido, looked towards Canelli and Calamandrana, towards Calosso, too, and felt as if I had been drinking wine, and become someone else, as if I was like Nuto and every bit as good as him, and that one fine day I'd take that train, too, and set out on my travels.

I'd been as far as Canelli several times by bicycle and I used to stop on the bridge over the Belbo—but the time I met Nuto there was like the very first time of all. He had come to get a horse-shoe for his father and saw me in front of the tobacconist's looking at the postcards. "So they let you have these cigarettes already?" he said unexpectedly at my back. And I who was working out how many coloured marbles you got for two *soldi* was ashamed of myself, and from that day I never touched them again. Then we walked about together and watched the people going in and out of the cafés. The cafés at Canelli aren't inns and you don't drink wine there but soft drinks. We listened to the young men talking about what they had done and telling the tallest of stories with the utmost calm. In the window there was a printed poster with a ship and white birds on it and even without asking Nuto I knew it was meant for the people who wanted to travel and see the world. Then we talked about it and he told me that one of these young men—he had fair hair and a tie and his trousers were neatly pressed—was clerk in the bank where the people who wanted to go on board ship got themselves fixed up. Another thing I heard that day was that at Canelli there was a carriage which every so often went out with three or even four women in it and these women drove through the streets or went as far as the station, to Sant' Anna and down the main road and they had a drink in various places—all this to let themselves be seen and attract customers. It was their boss who had thought it out and anyone who had the money and was old enough went into the house at Villanova and slept with one of them.

"Do all the women in Canelli do that?" I asked when I had understood what he meant.

"It would be better that way, but they don't," he said. "They don't all go about in a carriage."

There came a time with Nuto when I was sixteen or seventeen and he was going away to do his military service when the two of us would pinch a bottle from the cellar and take it up Salto; there we used to get among the reeds if it was by day or sit at the end of the vineyard if it was moonlight. And we drank from the bottle and talked about girls. The thing I hadn't grasped at that time was that all women are the same—they are all looking for a man. Yet it must be like that, I would say as I turned it over in my mind—but that all of them, even the prettiest, even the most ladylike, should like that sort of thing, amazed me. I had my wits about me more by this time and had heard plenty and I knew—because I had seen it—how even Irene and Silvia ran after the men. Still it amazed me. Then Nuto would say: "What do you expect? It's the same moon for everyone, like the rain or sickness. It doesn't matter whether they live in a hole in the ground or in a fine house, blood is red everywhere."

"But what does the priest say—that it's a sin?"

"It's a sin on Fridays," said Nuto, wiping his mouth, "but there are the other six days."

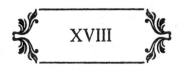

XVIII

I TOOK my share of the work and now Cirino sometimes listened to what I said about some farm or other and agreed with me. It was he who spoke to Sor Matteo and told him they must do something about me; if they wanted to keep me about the place and make me take some interest in the harvest instead of running off bird-nesting with the other boys, I'd have to be taken on as a day-labourer. So now I was hoeing and spraying the vines and ploughing and getting to know my way about with the farm animals. I could put my back into it, too. Off my own bat, I'd learnt to graft, and the apricot tree, which is still in the garden, I'd grafted myself on to a plum. Sor Matteo called me on to the terrace one day—Silvia and the Signora were there, too—and asked me what had become of Padrino. Silvia was sitting in her deck chair and looking away over the top of the lime trees and the Signora was knitting. Silvia was black-haired and dressed in red; she wasn't so tall as Irene, but both of them were better dressed than their step-mother. They must have been twenty at least. When they walked past with their parasols, I eyed them from the vineyard the way you look at a couple of peaches too high on the branch. When they came to gather the grapes with us, I ran off into Emilia's row and whistled away by myself from there.

I said I hadn't seen Padrino again and asked him why he had called me. I was vexed because my trousers were covered with copper-sulphate and I'd some splashes of it on my face, too. I hadn't expected to find the women there. When I think about it now, it's clear that Sor Matteo did it on purpose to embarrass me, but to make myself feel braver I kept thinking about something Emilia had told us about Silvia: "As for her! She sleeps without a nightdress."

"You're such a worker," Sor Matteo said to me that day, "and you've gone and let Padrino ruin his vineyard. Aren't you ashamed of yourself?"

"They're still boys," said the Signora, "and they're asking to be taken on by the day already!"

I could have sunk into the floor. Silvia looked round from her deck-chair and said something to her father.

"Has anyone gone to get the seeds from Canelli yet?" she said. "The pinks are out already at Il Nido."

No one said, "Go yourself then." But, instead, Sor Matteo looked at me for a moment and muttered:

"Is the vineyard with the green grapes finished yet?"

"We'll finish it tonight."

"Tomorrow there's that waggon to be done."

"The grieve said he would see to it."

Sor Matteo looked at me again and said I was hired by the day with board and lodgings and that should be enough for me. "The horse puts up with it," he said, "and it works harder than you do. The oxen put up with it, too. Do you remember, Elvira, when this boy came, he was like a sparrow? Now he's putting on flesh, he's getting as fat as a friar. If you're not careful," he said, "we'll kill you with the pig at Christmas."

"Is no one going to Canelli?" Silvia said.

"Tell him to go," said her stepmother. Santina and Emilia came out on to the terrace. Santina had little red shoes and soft hair, so fair that it was nearly white; she wouldn't eat her bread and milk and Emilia was trying to catch her and carry her into the house.

"Santa Santina," said Sor Matteo, getting up, "come here and let me eat you up."

While they were making a fuss of the child, I didn't know whether to go away or not. The window of the room was shining and when I looked away beyond the Belbo, I saw Gaminella and the reed-bed and the water-course at my home. I remembered the five lire from the town council.

Then I said to Sor Matteo who was bouncing the child up and down:

"Have I to go to Canelli tomorrow?"

"Ask her."

But Silvia was leaning over the parapet shouting to someone to wait for her. Irene was passing in the gig under the pine tree with another girl, and a young man from the Station was driving them.

"Will you take me to Canelli?" shouted Silvia.

A moment later they had all gone. Signora Elvira had gone back into the house with the little girl and the others went laughing along the road.

I said to Sor Matteo: "Once the orphanage used to pay out five lire for me. It's a while since I've seen it and who knows who's getting it? But my work's worth more than five lire. I must get some shoes."

I was happy that night and I told Cirino and Nuto and Emilia and the horse. Sor Matteo had promised to give me fifty lire a month, all to myself. Serafina asked me if I wanted her to keep my money for me—I'd lose it if I kept it in my pocket. She asked me when Nuto was there and he began to whistle and said that four *soldi* in the hand were better than a million in the bank. Then Emilia began to say she wanted a present from me and they talked about my money all night.

But, as Cirino said, now that I was fixed up, it was up to me to work like a man. I hadn't changed at all—I had the same arms and the same back and they still called me Anguilla, I couldn't understand the difference. Nuto advised me not to stand for it; he said that probably if they were giving me fifty, my work would be worth a hundred and why shouldn't I buy an ocarina.

"I couldn't learn to play it," I told him. "It's no use. I was born like that."

"It's so easy," he said.

I had another idea. I was thinking that, if I had that money, I'd be able to leave here some fine day.

Instead, the money I earned in the summer, I squandered the whole lot at the fair, at the shooting-booth and other silly things. It was then I bought myself a clasp-knife, the one I frightened the boys from Canelli with the night they waited for me on the road to Sant' Antonio. If you walked about the streets a bit too often and had a good look round you in those days the end of it was they waited for you with a handkerchief tied round one fist. And once, said the old people, it had been even worse—once they used to kill each other and people were knifed—on the road from Camo there was still the cross at an overhanging place on the road where they had capsized a gig with two people in it. But now the government had seen to that with its policy of making everybody live at peace—there had been the time of the fascists who had beaten up anybody they wanted and the *carabinieri* had known all about it and everybody had watched his step. The old folks said it was better now.

In this respect, too, Nuto had his wits about him more than I had. By this time he was going about all over the countryside and could argue with anyone. That winter, even, when he was courting a girl at S. Anna and came and went by night, no one ever said anything to him. Maybe it was because round about this time he began to play the clarinet and everyone knew his father and because he always gave a good account of himself at the game of *pallone*—anyway, he was allowed to go about and crack jokes without anyone taking any notice. He knew a good few people at Canelli and when he heard they wanted to take it out of someone, he called them all sorts of fools and told them to leave the job to people who were paid for it. He made them think shame of themselves. He told them it was only dogs that bark and go for strange dogs, and men set on a dog because it suits them to show that they are still masters, but if the dogs weren't dumb animals they would come to an agreement with each other and start barking at them. Where he had got these ideas from I don't know, unless from his father or from some tramp; he said it was like the war which had been fought in 1918—a whole pack of dogs un-leashed by the masters so that they would kill each other and the masters be left in command. You only needed to read the papers that came out then to understand that the world is full of people who set on their dogs. I often remember this saying of Nuto's on days when I don't want to know any more what is happening and have only to walk along the streets to see people with papers in their hands and the headlines as black as thunder-clouds.

Now that I had my first pay, I felt I wanted to know how Angiolina and Giulia and Padrino were getting on. But I never had a chance to go and see them. I asked the people from Cossano who passed by on the main road during the grape harvest, taking the cartloads of grapes to Canelli. One of them came to tell me once that they were ex-pecting me, that Giulia was expecting me, and that they weren't forgetting me. I asked him how the girls were now.

"What girls?" he said. "They're a couple of women now. They work by the day like you do."

Then I really made up my mind to go to Cossano but I never found time and in winter the road was too bad.

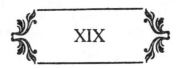

XIX

ON THE first market-day Cinto came to the inn to get the knife I had promised him. I was told a small boy was waiting for me outside and I found him dressed in his Sunday-best, with his little clogs, watching four men playing cards. His father, he said, was in the square, looking at a hoe.

"Do you want the money or the knife?" I asked him. He wanted the knife. Then we came out into the sun and passed between the rows of stalls piled with cloth and water-melons, through the crowd of people and past the sacking stretched on the ground covered with horse-shoes and hooks and ploughshares and nails, and we looked for a knife.

"If your father sees it," I told him, "I wouldn't put it past him to take it from you. Where will you hide it?"

Cinto laughed, with those strange eyes of his, without lashes. "My father——" he said. "If he takes it from me, I'll kill him."

At the stall with the knives, I told him to choose one. He didn't believe I was in earnest. "Come on. Hurry up." He chose a knife that made even my mouth water; it was fine and big and the handle was chestnut-coloured, with two spring-blades and a corkscrew.

Then we went back to the inn and I asked him if he had found any more playing cards in the ditches. He was holding the knife in his hand and trying the blades against his palm. He said he hadn't. I told him I had once bought myself a knife like that at the Canelli market and had used it to cut willows with when I was on the farm.

I got them to give him a glass of peppermint, and while he was drinking it, I asked him if he had ever been in the train or the bus. He said that he'd rather have gone on a bicycle but Gosto from Il Morone had told him it was impossible with his foot as it was, it would have had to be a motor-cycle. I started to tell him that I went about in a truck when I was in California, and he stood there listening to me without another glance at the four who were playing *tarocchi*.

Then he said, "There's a match today," and his eyes widened.

I was just going to say, "And aren't you going?" when Valino appeared at the door of the inn, a black look on his face. The boy heard him, if indeed he wasn't aware of him even before he saw him, and he put down his glass and went off with his father. They disappeared together into the sunshine.

What would I have given to see the world still through Cinto's eyes, to start again in Gaminella like him, with the same father, with the same leg even—now that I knew so much and was able to look after myself. It wasn't that I felt sorry for him, sometimes I envied him. I seemed to know even the dreams he dreamt at nights and the thoughts that passed through his mind as he hobbled about the square. I hadn't walked like that, I wasn't lame, but how often had I seen the carts rumbling past, with crowds of women and children on top, going to the fair, to the merry-go-rounds at Castiglione, at Cossano, at Campetto, all over the countryside, and I stayed behind with Giulia and Angiolina these long summer evenings, under the hazels, under the fig tree, on the parapet of the bridge, looking at the sky and the vineyards which never changed. And then at night, all night long, we heard them coming back along the road, singing and laughing and calling to each other across the Belbo. On nights like these, if I saw a light or a bonfire on the distant hills, it would make me cry out and roll over on the cold ground, because I was poor, because I was a child, because I was nothing at all. I was almost pleased if a storm came and spoiled the festa, one of these summer storms, like the crack of doom. I think longingly of these days when I look back on them now and wish I could be a boy again.

And I wished I could be in the farmyard at La Mora again that August afternoon when they had all gone to the fair at Canelli, even Cirino, even the neighbours, and, because I had only clogs, they had said to me, "You don't want to go without shoes. Stay and look after the farm." It was the first year I was at La Mora and I didn't dare to rebel. But for a while I'd looked forward to that fair—Canelli had always been famous, there was the greasy pole, and the sack-race and the game at *pallone*.

Sor Matteo and his wife and daughters had gone, too, and the baby with Emilia in the big carriage and the house was locked up. I was left alone with the dog and the oxen. I stayed for a while behind the garden gate, watching the passers-by. They were all going to Canelli. I envied even the beggars and the cripples. Then I began to throw stones at the dove-cote to break the tiles and I heard them fall and rebound on the cement of the terrace. To vent my ill-temper on something, I took the bill-hook and ran off into the fields. So I'm *not* looking after the house, I thought. Who cares if the house catches fire or if it's broken into? In the fields I didn't hear the chatter of the passers-by any more and that made me even more angry and frightened, so that I nearly cried. I started to hunt grasshoppers and tore off their legs, breaking them off at the joint. "Too bad for you," I said to them. "You should have gone to Canelli." And I shouted and swore, using all the bad words I knew.

If I dared, I would have laid waste every flower in the garden. And I thought of the faces of Irene and Silvia and told myself that even they made water, too.

A gig stopped at the gate.

"Is there anyone at home?" I heard them calling. It was two officers from Nizza whom I had once seen on the terrace with them. I stayed hidden behind the porch and didn't say a word. "Is there anyone at home, young ladies?" they shouted. "Signorina Irene!" The dog started to bark, but I kept quiet.

After a little while they went away and I was pleased about it. They're bastards, too, I thought. I went into the house to get a bit of bread to eat. The cellar was locked. But on the flat top of the cupboard among the onions there was a bottle of good wine and I took it and went off to drink it all up behind the dahlias. My head was going round now and buzzing as if it were full of flies. I went back into the room and broke the bottle on the floor, to look as if the cat had done it, and poured out a little of the poor wine to pretend it was that I had drunk.

I stayed drunk till the evening and I was drunk when I watered the oxen and changed the litter and flung down the fresh hay. People began to pass along the road again and from behind the gate I asked what had been hung at the top of the greasy pole and if the race had really been run in sacks and who had won it. They were glad to stop and speak, no one had ever spoken so much to me. Now I felt quite different and I was downright sorry I hadn't spoken to the two officers and asked them what they wanted with our girls and if they really thought they were the same as the ones at Canelli.

When the people began to come back to La Mora, I knew enough about the fair to discuss it with Cirino and Emilia, with all of them, as if I had been there myself. At supper there was more to drink. The big carriage came back very late at night after I had been asleep for a while and was dreaming about climbing up Silvia's smooth back as if it was the greasy pole and I heard Cirino getting up to go to the gate and the sound of talking and doors banging and the horse snorting. I turned over on my mattress and thought how fine it was now that we were all here. The next morning we would wake up and go out into the farmyard and I'd still be talking about the fair and hear them talking about it.

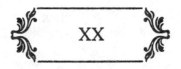

XX

To ME the best about these days was that everything was done in its season, and each season had its own customs and its own games which varied according to the work and the harvests and the rain or the fine weather. In winter we came into the kitchen with our clogs heavy with earth, our hands skinned and our shoulders almost broken with the plough, but when we had turned over the stubble fields there was no more work to be done and the snow fell. We spent so long eating chestnuts and sitting up late at night and walking about the stables that it seemed always Sunday. I remember—it was the last job of the winter and the first again after the blackbird came—those black wet heaps of leaves and millet we kindled, which smouldered in the fields, speaking of dark nights when we would sit late or promising fine weather for the morrow.

Winter was Nuto's season. Now that he was a young man and played the clarinet, he went about among the hills in summer or played at the Station, only in winter was he always near-by, in his own house or at La Mora, or in the farmyards. He used to turn up with his cyclist's beret and his old army pullover and start telling stories—that they had invented a machine to count the pears on the tree, that at Canelli thieves from outside the town had robbed the urinal during the night, that so-and-so at Calosso put muzzles on his children before he went out so that they wouldn't bite each other. He knew everyone's affairs. He knew there was a man at Cassinasco who, after he had sold his grapes, spread out the hundred lire notes on a drying tray and kept them there in the sun for an hour so that they wouldn't go bad. He knew of another man at Cumini who had a rupture as big as a pumpkin and asked his wife one day to try and milk him, too. He knew the story of the two men who had eaten a billy-goat, and afterwards one started to caper and bleat and the other went about butting. He told tales of brides, and broken marriages, and farms with a corpse in the cellar.

From the autumn until January the children played at marbles and the men at cards. Nuto knew all the games but the one he liked best was hiding the card and getting you to guess where it was, and making it come out of the pack by itself or pulling it out of a rabbit's ear. But when he came into the farmyard in the morning and found me on the threshing-floor in the sunshine, he used to break his cigarette in two and we lit up; then he said: "Now let's go and have a look under the roof." Under the roof meant in the turret of the dove-cote, an attic which you got to up the big stairs, past the landing where the family stayed, and where you had to keep bent down. Up there was a trunk, and a pile of broken springs and little heaps of horse-hair and other junk. A little round window which looked out on the hill at Salto seemed to me like the window at Gaminella. Nuto rummaged in the trunk; it was full of torn books and old rust-coloured pages and household accounts and broken pictures. He went through the books, banging them together to shake off the mould but even touching them for a little while made your hands icy cold. It was all stuff belonging to Sor Matteo's people, to his father who had studied at Alba. There were some in Latin, like the missal, and others with black men and wild beasts, and that was how I came to know elephants and lions and whales. Some Nuto took and carried home under his jersey since, as he said, "Nobody's going to use them in any case."

"What do you do with them?" I had asked him. "Don't you buy newspapers as it is?"

"They're books," he said, "read what you can of them. You'll never be anything if you don't read books."

As we crossed the landing we heard Irene playing the piano; on some fine sunny mornings the window was open and the sound of the piano came out on to the terrace among the lime trees. It always seemed strange to me that a piece of furniture that was so big and black with a sound that shook the windows should be played by Irene herself with her long white lady's hands. But play it she did and very well, too, according to Nuto. She had learned to play the piano in Alba when she was a little girl. But the one who banged away at the piano just to make a noise, and sang and then stopped in a temper was Silvia. Silvia was a year or two younger and she still ran up the stairs sometimes; she learnt to go on a bicycle this year and the station-master's son held her saddle for her.

When I heard the piano, I sometimes looked at my

hands and realised that between me and the gentry, between me and the ladies, there was a fine difference. Even now, when I haven't done any heavy work for almost twenty years and can write my name better than I had ever thought I would, if I look at my hands, I realise that I'm not a *signore* and that anyone can see I've had a hoe in my hand. But I've learnt that women don't mind that, either.

Nuto had said to Irene that she played like a professional and he could listen to her all day long. And Irene had called him on to the terrace then (I had gone with him, too), and with the window open had played difficult pieces, really lovely ones, whose sound filled the house, and which must have been heard as far as the vineyard with the green grapes which was beside the road. I enjoyed it, I can tell you. Nuto listened with his lips pursed up as if he had put the clarinet to his mouth, and through the window I saw the flowers in the room, and the mirrors and Irene's straight back and the effort of her arms, and her fair hair against the page. And I saw the hill and the vineyards and the watercourses and I realised that this music wasn't the same as the stuff the band played, it spoke of other things, it wasn't meant for Gaminella, nor the trees beside the Belbo nor for us. But in the distance towards Canelli you could see Il Nido against the outline of Salto, the fine red house, set among the yellowing plane trees. And the music Irene played went with the fine house, with the gentry at Canelli, it was meant for them.

"No," cried Nuto at one point, "that was wrong!" Irene had already corrected herself and started playing again, but she bent her head and looked at him for a moment, laughing and almost blushing. Then Nuto went into the room and turned over the pages for her and they talked about the music while Irene went on playing. I stayed on the terrace and kept on looking at Il Nido and Canelli.

These two daughters of Sor Matteo were not for me and not even for Nuto. They were rich and tall and beautiful. They went about with officers and surveyors, with the gentry and with young men in their twenties.

There was always someone amongst us in the evening, either Emilia or Serafina or Cirino, who knew who was courting Silvia now, who the letters Irene wrote were for, and who had escorted them the evening before. And they said that their stepmother didn't want to marry them off, didn't want to see them leave home, taking the farms with them as their dowry, but that she was trying to make the dowry for her own child, Santina, as big as she could. "Yes," said the grieve, "keep them in order. Two girls like that!"

I didn't say anything, and sometimes on a summer day, sitting beside the Belbo, I thought of Silvia. I didn't dare think of Irene with the fair hair. But one day when Irene had come to let Santina play in the sand and there wasn't anyone there, I saw them run and stop at the water's edge. I stayed hidden behind an elder tree. Santina cried out and pointed to something on the opposite bank. And then Irene had laid aside the book and bent down, taking off her stockings and shoes, and kilting her dress above her knees, showing her white legs—she was so fair-skinned—she went into the water. She crossed the river slowly, feeling each step first with her feet. Then, calling to Santina not to move, she picked some yellow flowers. I remember it as if it were yesterday.

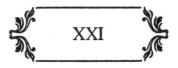

XXI

A few years later at Genoa where I was doing my military service, I had found a girl who was like Silvia; she was dark like her, but plumper and less straightforward, the same age as Irene and Silvia were when I started at La Mora. I was batman to the colonel who had a house beside the sea and had given me the job of looking after the garden. I kept the garden tidy, kindled the stoves and heated the bath water and was in and out of the kitchen. Teresa was the housemaid and made fun of the way I talked. That was why I had become a batman, so that I wouldn't have the sergeants always round about me, taking a loan of me whenever I opened my mouth. I looked her straight in the face—I've always done that—and didn't answer, but just kept looking at her. I listened carefully to what people said, I didn't speak much, and I learnt something every day.

Teresa would laugh and ask me if I hadn't a girl to wash my shirts for me.

"Not at Genoa," I said.

Then she wanted to know if I took a bundle home with me when I went on leave to the village.

"I'm not going back to the village," I said. " I want to stay here in Genoa."

"What about the girl?"

"It doesn't matter," I said. "There are girls in Genoa, too."

She would smile and ask Who, for instance? Then I laughed, too, and said, I don't know.

When she became my girl and I used to go up the stairs at night to get her in her cubby-hole and make love, she always asked me what I was going to do in Genoa without a trade, and why I didn't want to go home. She said it half in fun and half in earnest. "Because you are here," I could have said to her, but there was no need for we were in the bed already, in each other's arms. Or else tell her that even Genoa wasn't enough, that Nuto had been in Genoa, too, that they all came here—I was fed-up with Genoa by now and wanted to go further afield—but if I had told her that she would have flown into a temper, and taken my hands and started to curse me because even I was like the rest. "But the others," I would have explained, "don't mind staying in Genoa, that's why they come here. I have a trade, but nobody wants it in Genoa. I must go to a place where my trade brings me some return. But it's got to be far away where no one from my village has ever been."

Teresa knew I was a bastard and kept asking me why I didn't have searches made; if I wasn't anxious to find out my mother's name at least. "Maybe," she said, "it's your blood that makes you like this. You're a gipsy's son, you've got curly hair."

(Emilia, who had given me my nickname of *Anguilla*,

the Eel, always used to say I must be the son of a mounte-bank and a nanny-goat.) I laughed and said I was a priest's son. And even then Nuto had asked, "Why do you say that?" "Because he's a good-for-nothing," said Emilia. Then Nuto had shouted that no one is ever born a good-for-nothing, or wicked, or a criminal; people are all born the same and it's only other people who spoil what you started off with by treating you badly.

"Take Ganola," I retorted, "he's crazy; he was born that way."

"Crazy doesn't mean bad," said Nuto. "It's only stupid people shouting after him that make him angry."

I used to think about these things only when I had a woman in my arms. Some years later—I was in America by then—I realised that as far as I was concerned, the whole nation were bastards. Where I lived at Fresno I went to bed with a lot of women, I nearly married one of them, even, but I never managed to make out where their people were, or where they belonged. They lived alone; that one worked in a jam factory, this one in an office—Rosanne was a schoolmistress who had come from somewhere or other, from one of the grain states, with a letter for a film weekly, and she would never tell me what sort of life she had led on the coast. She would say only that it had been hard, *a hell of a time*. It had left her with a slightly hoarse voice. It is true that there were whole families of them, especially on the hill, in the new houses in front of the holdings and in the fruit-canning factories, and on summer evenings you heard the din and smelt the vines and figs in the air, and bands of boys and girls ran through the alleys and along the avenues, but these people were Americans and Mexicans and Italians who seemed always just to have arrived, and they lived on the land in the same way as the street-sweepers in the city cleaned the side-walks, and they slept in the city and found their amusements there. But where a man came from and who was his father or his grandfather I never got round to asking. And there were no country girls there. Even the ones from up the valley had no idea what a nanny-goat was or a watercourse. They rushed to their work in cars, on bicycles, and on trains, just like office girls. They did everything in gangs in the city, even the decoration of the floats for the grape festival.

During the months that Rosanne slept with me, I realised that she was a real bastard, that all she had were the legs she would stretch out on the bed, that maybe she had her old father and mother in one of the grain states, but only one thing mattered to her—to get me to go back with her to the coast and open an Italian bar, hung with vines (*A fancy place, you know*) in the hope that some-one would see her and take her photograph and have it printed in one of the coloured weeklies (*Only gimme a break, baby*). She was ready to be photographed naked, even, astride the fire-escape, as long as people got to know her. How she got it into her head that I could be of some use to her, I don't know. When I asked her why she came to bed with me, she laughed and said after all I was a man (*Put it the other way round, you come with me because I'm a girl*). And she wasn't stupid either, she knew what she wanted—only she wanted the impossible.

She never touched a drop of liquor (*Your looks, you know, are your only free advertising agent*) and when prohibition came in, it was she who advised me to make bootlegger's gin, for those who might still want it, and there were a lot of them.

She was a tall blonde, always smoothing out the lines in her face and setting her hair. If you hadn't known her, you would have said, when you saw her coming out of the school gate with that walk of hers, that she was a hard-working student. What she taught I don't know; the boys in her class greeted her by flinging their caps in the air and whistling. At first when I spoke to her, I hid my hands and disguised my voice. She asked me right away why I didn't become an American. "Because I'm not," I muttered; "because I'm a wop." And she laughed and said that it was money and brains that made you an American. "Which haven't you got?"

I have often wondered what sort of children might have come from the two of us, from her smooth, firm sides and that white belly she fed with milk and orange juice, and from me, from my thick blood. We both of us came from God knows where, and this was the only way of finding out who we were and what we really had in our veins. It would be fine, I thought, if my son were like my father or my grandfather and so I would see with my own eyes who I was at last. Rosanne would even have given me a son, if I had agreed to go to the coast. But I held back. I didn't want a little American boy—with me for father and Rosanne for mother, it would have been another bastard. By that time, I knew I would come back.

As long as she was with me, Rosanne didn't get anywhere. Sometimes in the summer we went to the coast by car on Sundays and bathed; she walked along the beach in her coloured wrap and sandals, sipping a soft drink at the swimming pool in her shorts, and then stretched herself out in a deck-chair, as if she was in my bed. I laughed, but at whom I'm not sure. And yet I liked the girl, she pleased me as the tang of the air does some mornings or the feel of the fresh fruit on the roadside stalls of the Italians.

Then one evening she told me she was going back home. I was astonished because I had never imagined she could do such a thing. I was just going to ask her how long she was going for, when she looked down at her knees—she was sitting beside me in the car—and said I wasn't to ask anything, it was all settled and she was going home for good. I asked her when she was leaving. "Tomorrow, perhaps. *Any time*."

While I was taking her back to the boarding-house, I said that we could get things straight and arrange to get married. Half-smiling she let me speak while she looked down at her knees and wrinkled her brow. "I've thought about it," she said in that hoarse voice of hers. "It's no use. It's all up. *I've lost my battle*."

Instead of going home, she went back to the coast again. But she never appeared in the coloured weeklies. Months afterwards she sent me a post-card from Santa Monica asking for money. I sent it to her but she didn't reply. I never heard any more about her.

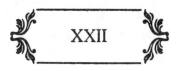

XXII

I'VE KNOWN a few women on my travels, fair ones and dark—I've gone after them and spent a pretty penny on them; now that I'm not young any more they come after me, but what does it matter—and I've realised that Sor Matteo's daughters weren't the prettiest after all—Santina, perhaps, but then I didn't see her when she grew up—they had the same beauty as dahlias, or roses, or the flowers that grow in gardens under the fruit trees. I've come to realise that they weren't very clever either, and that in spite of their piano-playing and their novels and their tea-drinking and their parasols, they couldn't manage their own lives—they weren't cut out to be real ladies and to lord it over a man and a house. There are plenty of peasant women in the valley who are better able to manage themselves and others, too. Irene and Silvia weren't peasants any more and they weren't real ladies yet, either. They didn't manage very well, poor things—that's how they died.

I saw this weakness of theirs far back, at one of the first grape harvests—I noticed it even if I didn't really understand it yet. All through the summer you had only to look up from the farmyard or from the fields and see the terrace and the big window and the tiled roof to remember that the house was theirs, it belonged to them and their stepmother and the little girl, and even Sor Matteo himself couldn't go into the room without wiping his feet on the mat. Sometimes you would hear them calling to each other up there, and you would have to tie up their horse for them and see them coming out of the glass doors and going for a walk with their parasols, so smart that Emilia herself found nothing to criticise. Some mornings one of them came down into the farm-yard, passing through between the hoes and carts and beasts, and went into the garden to gather roses. And sometimes they even came out into the fields, along the paths in their flimsy shoes, and spoke to Serafina and the grieve, were frightened by the oxen, and carried a fine basket to gather the early grapes. One evening after we had piled the sheaves of grain—it was the evening of San Giovanni and there were bonfires everywhere—they came out, too, to get some fresh air and listen to the girls singing. And then when we were by ourselves in the kitchen or between the rows of vines, I heard all sorts of things about them, how they played the piano and read books and embroidered cushions and in church had their names on the seat. Well, at the time of this grape harvest, when the rest of us were preparing the baskets and wooden pails and cleaning out the cellar, and even Sor Matteo was walking about the vineyards, we heard from Emilia that the whole house was in a turmoil, that Silvia was slamming the doors, and Irene was sitting red-eyed at table without eating anything. I didn't understand what could be wrong with them. After all, there was the wine-making and all the fun of picking the grapes—to think that everything was being done for *them*, to fill the cellars and Sor Matteo's pockets, and that it was all theirs. One night Emilia told us what was the matter, when we were sitting on the beam. It was about Il Nido.

It so happened that the old countess—the countess from Genoa—who had come back from the seaside a fortnight ago to Il Nido with her daughters-in-law and grandchildren, had sent out invitations to Canelli and the Station for a party under the plane trees, and she had forgotten La Mora, forgotten the two of them, forgotten Signora Elvira. Forgotten, or had she done it on purpose. The three women made Sor Matteo's life a misery. Emilia said Santina was the least bad-tempered in the house now. "You'd think I'd killed somebody," said Emilia. One of them answers back, the other jumps up and the third slams the door. If they don't like it they can lump it.

Then the grape harvest came and I didn't think about them any more. That one fact was enough to open my eyes. Even Irene and Silvia were people like ourselves who turned bad-tempered when they were crossed, and would take offence and be sorry about it afterwards, and wanted what they hadn't got. Not all the gentry have the same standing—there are some more important than others, and some richer than others, who didn't even send out invitations to my mistresses. And then I began to wonder what the garden and the rooms at Il Nido must be like, if Irene and Silvia were dying to go there and couldn't get. We knew only what Tomasino and some of the farm labourers said because all that side of the hill was fenced round and a water-course separated it from our vineyards, where not even the hunters were allowed—there was a notice put up. And when you looked up from the main road below Il Nido you saw a clump of queer-looking canes which they called bamboo. Tomasino used to say there was a park, and round about the house a great lot of gravel, smaller and whiter than the stuff the roadman flung on the road in spring.

Then the land belonging to Il Nido stretched over the hill behind, vines and grain, grain and vines, and farms, and clumps of walnut trees and cherries and almonds as far as Sant'Antonio and beyond, and from there the land fell away to Canelli.

I had seen some of the flowers from Il Nido the year before, when Irene and Signora Elvira had gone there together and had come back with bunches which were more beautiful than the stained glass windows in the church or the priest's vestments. The year before, you might meet the old lady's carriage on the road to Canelli. Nuto had seen it and said that Moretto, the manservant who was driving, looked like a *carabiniere*, with his shiny cap and white tie. The carriage had never stopped at our house, it had passed only once to go to the Station. The old lady even heard mass at Canelli. And the old ones amongst us would say that a long time ago, before the old lady's time, the gentry at Il Nido didn't go even to hear mass, but heard it in the house, where they kept a priest who said mass every day in one of the rooms. But all this happened when the old lady was still a dowerless girl of no family and she and the count's son were courting in Genoa. Then she became the mistress of it all, for the count's son died, and a handsome officer that the old lady had married in France died, too, and so did their sons, somewhere or other, and now the old lady with white hair and a yellow parasol went to Canelli in her carriage and kept her grandchildren and gave them houseroom. But in the days when the count's son was alive and the French officer, Il Nido was always lit up at night, always gay, and the old lady, who at that time was still as fresh as a rose, gave dinner parties and balls and invited people from Nizza and Alessandria. Beautiful women came, and officers, and members of Parliament, all with their carriages and pairs and their servants, and played cards and ate ices and made merry.

Irene and Silvia knew all this and to be well treated by the old lady, received and fêted by her meant as much to them as it did to me to peep from the terrace into the room with the piano or to know that they were sitting at table over our heads and to see Emilia mimic them with a fork and spoon. Only, being women, they suffered because of the slight. And then they spent the whole day frittering away their time on the terrace or in the garden —they hadn't any work to do, any job to occupy themselves—they didn't even like looking after Santina. And so it was natural that their longing to leave La Mora and get into that park under the plane trees and be with the countess's daughters-in-law and grandchildren drove them to distraction—just as I felt when I saw the bonfires on the hill at Cassinasco or heard the train whistling through the night.

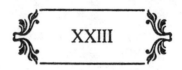

XXIII

THEN CAME the season when shots resounded early in the morning among the trees along the Belbo and on the hillside and Cirino began to tell us how he had seen the hare disappearing along a furrow. And that's the best time of the whole year. Gathering the grapes and stripping the leaves and pressing the fruit isn't really work at all, and it's not hot any more, and not cold yet; there are a few white clouds and you eat rabbit and polenta and go to look for mushrooms.

We farm-hands at La Mora went to gather mushrooms close by, but Irene and Silvia arranged with the other girls and young men they knew at Canelli to go in the gig as far as Agliano. They set off one morning when the mist was still lying in the meadows; I harnessed the horse, for they had to meet the others in the square at Canelli. The doctor's son from the Station took the whip, the one who always hit the bull's-eye at the shooting-booth and played cards all night long. That day a great storm got up with thunder and lightning like we have in August. Cirino and Serafina said it was better if it hailed now on the mushrooms and the people who were gathering them instead of on the harvest a fortnight before. The deluge of rain never stopped even during the night. Sor Matteo came to waken us with the lantern and his cloak over his head and told us to listen carefully for the gig coming back; he was worried. Upstairs, all the windows were lit up; Emilia ran upstairs and down making coffee and the little girl was screaming because they hadn't taken her to gather mushrooms, too.

The gig came back the next morning with the doctor's son flourishing the whip and shouting, "Hurrah for the rain at Agliano!"; he jumped down without touching the step and helped the two girls to alight; they were very cold and had scarves on their heads and empty baskets on their knees. They went upstairs and I heard them talking and laughing and getting warm.

After the excursion to Agliano, the doctor's son would often come along the road beneath the terrace and call to the girls and they would talk away together. Then in the winter afternoons they asked him to come in and he slapped his boots with his cane (for he went about in long hunting-boots) and looked all about him, broke off a flower or a twig—or, if he could find one, a red leaf from a young vine—and through the glass which closed it in we could see him climb quickly up the staircase. Upstairs there was a fine fire blazing up the chimney and you would hear them playing the piano and laughing until it was night. Sometimes Arturo stayed to supper. Emilia said they gave him tea and biscuits and Silvia always passed them to him, but it was Irene he was after. Irene, so fair-haired and well brought-up, began to play the piano so that she wouldn't have to speak to him, and Silvia lolled back on the sofa, soft and uncorseted, and the two of them chattered away together. Then the door opened and Signora Elvira chased in Santina, and Arturo got to his feet and said Good evening in a disappointed voice. "Here's another jealous young lady who wants to be introduced," said the Signora. Then Sor Matteo came in—he couldn't stand Arturo, but Signora Elvira went out of her way to be nice to him and thought that Arturo was an excellent match for Irene. It was Irene who had no use for him because she said he wasn't straight—he didn't even listen to the music and couldn't behave himself properly at table and only played with Santina to get on the right side of her mother. But Silvia took his part and got red and angry. For a while Irene was cool and self-possessed and said, "You can have him, why don't you take him?"

"Throw him out of the house," Sor Matteo said. "A man who gambles and hasn't a bit of land to his name is no man at all."

Towards the end of the winter Arturo began to bring a clerk from the Station with him, a friend of his, very tall and thin, and he attached himself to Irene, too. He only spoke Italian, not dialect, but he knew about music. This long drink of water began to play duets with Irene, and when they saw the two of them paired off together like this, Arturo and Silvia put their arms round each other to dance and they laughed to each other and now when Santina came in, it was the friend's turn to throw her up in the air and catch her again as she fell.

"If it weren't that he comes from Tuscany," Sor Matteo would say, "I'd call him a fool. The airs he puts on. . . . There was a man from Tuscany serving with us in Tripoli."

I knew what the room looked like with the two bunches of flowers and red leaves on the piano, the curtains sewn by Irene and the transparent marble lamp hung from a chain, which gave a light like the moon reflected in water. Some evenings they muffled themselves up, all four of them, and came out on to the terrace in the snow. Here the two men would smoke a cigar, and then if you stayed beneath the young vine with its withered leaves, you heard them talking.

Even Nuto came to hear what they said. The best thing of all was to hear Arturo showing off and telling how many people he had pushed off the train at Castiglione the other day or about that time at Acqui when he had staked his last penny and if he had lost he wasn't going home any more but he had won enough to pay for his supper instead. The man from Tuscany said, "Do you remember how you punched that man . . .?" And then Arturo told them how he'd punched him.

The girls sighed, leaning on the balustrade. The young man from Tuscany went over beside Irene and told her about his home and how he used to go and play the organ in the church. At a certain point the two cigars fell at our feet in the snow and then we heard them whispering up there and moving about and then came a sigh louder than the others. When we looked up we could see nothing but the withered vine leaves and thousands of stars in the frosty sky. Nuto said "The blackguards" through his clenched teeth.

I was always turning it over in my mind and I even asked Emilia about it, but I could never make out how they had hitched up. Sor Matteo only grumbled about

Irene and the doctor's son and said he'd give him a piece of his mind one day. The Signora made out that she was hurt, but Irene shrugged her shoulders and said she wouldn't have that boor Arturo even for a farm-hand, but she couldn't do anything about it if he came to visit her. Then Silvia said it was the man from Tuscany who was the fool and Signora Elvira pretended to be hurt again.

Irene couldn't carry on with the young man from Tuscany because Arturo kept an eye on them and he bossed his friend. So it must mean that Arturo was after them both, and, while he hoped to land Irene, amused himself with the other one. All you had to do was to wait for the good weather and go behind them through the fields and then you'd soon know.

But in the meantime Sor Matteo got a hold of this Arturo—we got the story from Lanzone who happened to be passing by the porch—and told him that women are women and men men. Isn't that right? Arturo who had just picked himself a buttonhole, tapped his boots with his riding-crop, and, sniffing the flowers, looked askance at Sor Matteo. "All right then," Sor Matteo went on; "when they are well brought-up, women know the kind of men they want to marry. And they don't want you," he said. "Do you get me?"

Then Arturo had muttered a lot, damn it all, they'd been kind enough to invite him to the house, naturally when a man . . .

"You're not a man," Sor Matteo had said, "you're a filthy so-and-so."

So the episode of Arturo seemed to be closed, and that

134

of the man from Tuscany, too. But the stepmother didn't have time to be hurt because other young men came, lots of others even more dangerous. The two officers, for instance, the ones who came the day I had stayed all by myself at La Mora. There was one month—there were fireflies, for it was June—when you saw them appearing every evening from Canelli. They must have had another woman who stayed along the main road because they never came from that direction but cut across from the Belbo over the footbridge and through the fields of millet and the meadows. I was sixteen at the time and beginning to understand all this. Cirino had a grudge against them because they trampled down his fodder, and he remembered besides what bastards officers like that had been in the war. And as for Nuto . . . One evening they played a dirty trick on them. They lay in wait for them coming through the grass and set a snare. The officers came along and jumped the ditch, looking forward to their evening with the young ladies, and fell headlong, splitting their faces open. It would have been a good joke to make them fall into the manure, but after that evening they didn't come through the fields again.

When the fine weather came there was no holding Silvia in. In the summer evenings they had started to come out of the gate and walk up and down with their young men on the road, and when they passed under the lime trees we pricked up our ears to catch a few words of what they said. The four of them started off together and they came back two and two. Silvia would walk arm in arm with Irene laughing and joking and talking impudently to the two men. When they passed back again into the scent of the lime trees, Silvia and her sweetheart were walking along together, whispering and laughing. The other pair came more slowly, walking a bit apart from each other, and sometimes they called to the pair in front and carried on a conversation with them in a loud voice. How well I remember these evenings, the farm-hands sitting on the cross-beam, among the strong, strong scent of the lime trees.

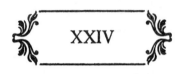

XXIV

LITTLE Santa, who was three or four at the time, was a sight worth seeing. Her hair was turning out golden like Irene's, and she had Silvia's black eyes, but if she bit her finger when she was eating an apple, or tore the heads off the flowers in a temper, or wanted us to lift her up on horseback whatever might happen and kept kicking us, we said she took it from her mother. Sor Matteo and his two daughters took things more calmly and weren't so overbearing. Irene was particularly calm; she was tall and always wore white and never got cross with anyone. She didn't need to, for when she asked for anything she always said please, even to Emilia, and to the rest of us, too, looking at us while she spoke, looking us right in the eyes. Even Silvia looked at us that way, too, but she wasn't so cool or so frank. The last years I was at La Mora I was getting fifty lire and used to wear a tie at the festa, but I knew I had got there too late and I couldn't do anything now.

But not even during these last years had I dared to think of Irene. And Nuto wasn't concerned about her either because now he played the clarinet all round the countryside and had a girl at Canelli. The talk about Irene was that someone from Canelli was courting her, for they were always going there and buying things in the shops and giving their cast-off dresses to Emilia. But Il Nido was opened up again and there was a supper party to which the Signora and her daughters were invited and that day the dressmaker came from Canelli to dress them. I drove them in the gig as far as the bend on the hill and I heard them talking about the big houses in Genoa. They told me to come back for them at midnight and to come right into the courtyard of Il Nido—in the dark the other guests wouldn't see that the upholstery of the gig was shabby. They told me to put my tie on straight, too, so that I wouldn't look a sight.

But at midnight when I came into the courtyard among the other carriages—seen from below the house was enormous and the shadows of the guests passed across the wide-open windows—no one showed up and I was left there among the plane trees for a good while. When I got fed-up listening to the crickets—there were crickets even up there—I climbed down from the gig and made my way to the door. In the first room I found a girl in a white apron who looked at me and made off. Then she came back and I said that I had come. She asked me what I wanted and I said that the gig for La Mora was waiting.

A door opened and I heard the sound of laughter. There were pictures of flowers on all the doors in this room and on the floor gleaming patterns in stone. The girl came back and told me I could go away because someone would accompany the ladies home.

When I was outside again I was sorry I hadn't taken a better look at that room which was more beautiful than a church. I led the horse over the gravel which crunched under its hooves beneath the plane trees and looked at them against the sky—seen from below it didn't seem a wood any longer but each tree made its own archway of shade—and at the gate I lit a cigarette and came down the road slowly among the bamboo and acacias and the gnarled trunks, thinking what sort of a stuff it is, this earth, that bears all kinds of trees.

Someone in the big house must have been courting Irene because I heard Silvia sometimes making fun of her and calling her "your ladyship", and soon Emilia got to know that the man had about as much life in him as a corpse, one of the crowd of grandsons the old lady kept purposely at arm's length so that they wouldn't eat her out of house and home. This grandson, this poor relation, this little count, never deigned to come to La Mora, but he sometimes sent a barefoot boy to carry letters to Irene telling her he was waiting at the side of the road to go for a walk. And Irene went.

From among the beans in the kitchen garden where I was watering them or tying them up, I heard Irene and Silvia sitting under the magnolia tree talking about it.

Irene was saying, "Well, what about it? The countess

is very particular. A boy like him can't possibly go to the festa at the Station. He'd find himself among his own servants."

"And what's the harm in that? He meets them in the house every day in life."

"She doesn't want him to go hunting either. You know his father died that way, it was tragic."

"He could come and see you, anyway. Why doesn't he come?" said Silvia unexpectedly.

"*He* doesn't come, either, to see you here. Why doesn't he come? Be careful, Silvia. Are you sure he's telling you the truth?"

"No one tells the truth. If you think about the truth, you go off your head. Don't you go telling him now . . ."

"It's you that sees him," said Irene. "It's you that's taking the risk. I only hope he's not coarse like the other one."

Silvia laughed softly. I couldn't keep still for ever behind the beans, they would have noticed me. I struck the earth with my hoe and listened.

"Do you think he'll have heard?" Irene said.

"Not him, he's only the farm-boy," said Silvia.

But there was the time when Silvia was weeping, twisting about in her deck-chair and weeping. In the porch Cirino was hammering at a bit of iron and I couldn't hear. Irene stayed beside her and stroked her hair which Silvia had been tearing at with her nails. "No, no," wept Silvia, "I want to go away from here. I want to get away. I don't believe it, I don't believe it, I don't believe it."

I couldn't hear for Cirino and his damned bit of iron.

"Come," said Irene and touched her. "Come up on to the terrace and keep quiet."

"I don't care," wept Silvia. "Nothing matters any more."

Silvia was going about with someone from Crevalcuore, who had a bit of land at Calosso; he owned a sawmill and went about on a motor-cycle. Silvia climbed up behind and away they went along the main road. In the evening we would hear the noise of the motor-cycle stopping and then starting again, and after a bit Silvia would appear at the gate with her black hair in her eyes. Sor Matteo knew nothing about it.

Emilia said that this man wasn't the first, the doctor's son had had her already in his father's consulting room in his own house. But no one ever knew the truth of this; if Arturo had really been going to bed with her, why had they stopped in summer of all times, when the weather was getting better and it was easier to meet? Instead, the motor-cyclist had come on the scene and now everyone knew that Silvia behaved as if she had gone off her head and got him to take her among the reeds and up the watercourses; people would meet them at Canio or at Santa Libera or in the woods at Bravo. Sometimes they even went to the hotel at Nizza.

To look at, she was always the same with these dark burning eyes of hers. I don't know whether she hoped to get herself married, but this Matteo from Crevalcuore was a quarrelsome fellow, a woodcutter who had already hopped in and out of a good few beds, and no one had ever stopped him yet. "Now," I thought, "if Silvia has a child, it will be a bastard like me. That's how I was born."

Irene was worried about it, too. She must have tried to help Silvia and she knew more about it than we did. It was impossible to imagine Irene on the back of that motor-cycle or among the reeds with someone or lying in a watercourse. Santina, now, would be more likely, when she was bigger; everyone said she would do the same. Their stepmother didn't say anything, she only insisted that they came home at the proper time.

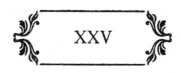

XXV

I NEVER saw Irene give way to despair as her sister did, but when two days passed without a summons to Il Nido, she kept just inside the garden gate, all on edge, or else took a book or her sewing and sat in the vineyard along with Santina, and from there she watched the road. When she set out with her parasol towards Canelli, then she was happy. What she found to say to this Cesarino who was about as lively as a corpse, I don't know; once when I passed pedalling like mad towards Canelli and caught a glimpse of them among the acacias, it looked as if Irene was standing reading a book while Cesarino was sitting on the bank in front of her looking at her.

One day Arturo, complete with riding-boots, had

turned up at La Mora; he had stopped beneath the terrace and spoken to Silvia, who was scanning the road from up there, but Silvia hadn't invited him to come up and had only said the day was close and these shoes with the low heels—she lifted a foot—you could get them at Canelli now.

Arturo had winked and had asked her if they still played dance music and if Irene still played the piano. "Ask her yourself," said Silvia, and looked away beyond the pine tree.

Irene hardly played at all now. It appears that there were no pianos at Il Nido and the old lady couldn't bear to see a girl wearing out her hands on the keyboard. When Irene went to visit the old lady, she took her bag with her sewing in it, a huge bag sewn with green flowers in wool, and in the bag she brought home books from Il Nido that the old lady had given her to read. They were old books bound in leather. In return she took illustrated fashion magazines—she sent to Canelli for them specially every week.

Serafina and Emilia said Irene was setting her cap at the count and that Sor Matteo had once said, "Be careful, girls. There are some old people who never die."

It was difficult to work out just how many relations the countess had at Genoa—it was even said there was a bishop among them. I had heard tell that the old lady didn't keep any staff now, either outdoors or in—she had enough grandsons and granddaughters. If that was how it was, I couldn't see what hope Irene had, for, however well the affair went, Cesarino would have to share with all these others. Unless Irene was prepared to content herself with being a servant at Il Nido. But when I looked round the farm, at the stable, the haylofts, the wheat, the grapes, I thought perhaps Irene was richer than he was and maybe Cesarino courted her to get his hand on her dowry. This idea, although it made me furious, was all the more attractive to me since it didn't seem possible that Irene could be so infatuated as to fling herself away merely because she was ambitious.

But then, I said, it's easily seen she's in love, that she likes Cesarino, that he's the man she's longing to marry. And I'd have liked to be able to speak to her, to tell her to be careful not to throw herself away on that half-baked creature, that fool who never emerged from Il Nido and sat on the ground while she read a book. Silvia, at least, didn't waste her time like that but went about with someone worth while. If it hadn't been that I was only the farm-boy and not eighteen yet, Silvia would perhaps have gone with me.

And Irene was having a bad time of it, into the bargain. This little so-and-so of a count must have been worse than a spoilt girl. He had tantrums and made her run after him and exploited the old lady's name shamelessly, and to everything Irene told him or asked him he answered no, that they would have to see, that they wouldn't have to make any false moves or forget who he was, or the state of his health, or his likes and dislikes. And now it was Silvia who had to listen to Irene's sighs on the few occasions when she didn't run off up the hillside or shut herself up in the house. At table, so Emilia said, Irene would sit with her eyes down and Silvia stared her father in the face as if she had a fever. Only Signora

Elvira talked on as dry as you please and wiped Santina's mouth, harping maliciously on the lost chances of the doctor's son, the man from Tuscany, the officers and the others, and about some girls in Canelli, younger than they were, who were married already and well on the way to having a christening. Sor Matteo muttered away, he never knew anything.

Meanwhile with Silvia it was the same old story. When she was not beyond herself with rage, and would stop in the farmyard or the vineyard, it was a pleasure to see her or hear her. Some days she had the gig harnessed and went off on her own to Canelli and drove it herself like a man. Once she asked Nuto if he would be going to play the clarinet at Buon Consiglio where they held the horse races, and she wanted more than anything to buy a saddle at Canelli and learn to ride a horse and race with the others. Lanzone, the grieve, had the job of explaining to her that a horse that pulls a gig has bad habits and can't race. Then it came out that Silvia wanted to go to Buon Consiglio to meet Matteo there and show him she could sit a horse, too.

This girl, we farm-hands said, was going to end up by dressing like a man and going round the fairs and walking the tightrope.

This very year there had appeared at Canelli a great booth in which there was a merry-go-round made up of motor-cycles which went round with a din worse than the threshing machine, and the tickets were given out by a fat red-haired woman, getting on for forty, who had her fingers covered with rings and smoked cigarettes. Wait and see, we said, when he's tired of her, Matteo di Crevalcuore will put Silvia in charge of a merry-go-round just like that. At Canelli they said, too, that when you paid for your ticket all you had to do was to put your hands down on the counter in such and such a way and the red-headed woman told you right off when you could come back and go into the caravan with the curtains and make love to her on the straw. But Silvia wasn't at that stage yet. For all that she seemed crazy, she was crazy for Matteo, but she was so beautiful and so healthy that many men would have married her even now.

There were the wildest goings-on. She and Matteo were going to a hut now in the vineyard at Seraudi, a half-ruined hut on the edge of a gully which the motor-cycle couldn't reach, but they used to walk and carry the rug and cushions. Neither at La Mora nor at Crevalcuore did Matteo let himself be seen with Silvia, not to save her good name at all but so that he wouldn't get involved and have to commit himself. He knew he didn't want to go on with it and in this way he saved his face.

I looked in Silvia's face for signs of what she and Matteo were doing together. When we started to harvest the grapes that September either she or Irene came into the vineyard with the green grapes, just as they had done in other years, and I crouched down under the vines and watched her, watched her hands feeling for the clusters, watched the curve of her flanks, her waist, her hair in her eyes, and, when she went down the path, how she walked, the spring in her step, the quick turn of her head—I knew all of her from top to toe, yet I could never say,

"Look, she's changed. Matteo's been here!" She was the same, she was Silvia.

The grape-harvest was the last merry-making for La Mora that year. On All-Saints' Day, Irene took to her bed; the doctor came from Canelli, the doctor came from the Station—Irene had typhus and was dying of it. They sent Santina to Alba with Silvia to stay with relations away from the risk of infection. Silvia didn't want to go at first but then she resigned herself to it. Emilia and the stepmother had plenty of running about. There was a stove always burning in the rooms upstairs, and they changed Irene's bedclothes twice a day; she was delirious and they gave her injections and she lost all her hair. We went back and forward to Canelli for medicine. Until one day a nun came into the courtyard and Cirino said, "She won't last till Christmas." The next day the priest came.

XXVI

WHAT IS left of it all, of our life at La Mora? For years afterwards, a gust of perfume from lime trees in the evening had been enough to make me feel a different being, to feel my real self, without quite knowing why. One thing I always think about is how many people there must be living in this valley and in the world, for that matter, and the very same things are happening to them now as happened to us then, and they don't know it and never give it a thought. Maybe there's a house with girls living in it, and old people and a little girl—and a boy like Nuto and a place like Canelli and a Station, and there's probably someone like me who wants to go away and make his fortune—and in summer they thresh the grain and gather the grapes, and they hunt in winter, and there's a terrace, too, and everything happens the way it happened to us. That's how things are. They haven't changed a bit, boys or women or the world. They don't carry parasols any more and on Sunday they go to the cinema instead of the festa, and they send their grain to the grain pool, and the girls smoke, and yet life is still the same and they don't know that one day they'll look round about them and for them, too, it will all be over. The first thing I said when

I got off the boat at Genoa among all the war-damaged houses was that each house, each courtyard, each terrace has meant something to someone and the thought of so many past years of life, so many memories vanished thus in the space of a night without leaving a trace is even more saddening than the material loss or the number of those who died. Or am I wrong? Maybe it's better like this, better that everything should go up in a blaze of dry grass and that people should begin again. This is what they do in America—when you're fed up with something, with a job or a place. Over there whole villages are empty now—the inn, the town hall and the shops, too—like a cemetery.

Nuto doesn't like to speak about La Mora but he asks me often if I really haven't seen anyone. He was thinking of the boys from round about, the people he played bowls and *pallone* with and met at the inn, and the girls we danced with. He knew where all of them were and what they'd done; when we were at his house on Salto and one of them passed along the road, Nuto asked him half-closing his eyes, "Do you still know who this is?" Then he would enjoy the other's expression of astonishment and pour out wine all round. We would talk away together. Someone used the formal "*voi*" to me. "I am Anguilla," I interrupted, "what nonsense is this? How did they die, your brother, your father, your grandmother? And is the bitch dead, too?"

They weren't much changed but I was changed. They recalled things I had said and done, jokes I had played, and blows, and stories I had forgotten. "And Bianchetta," one of them said to me, "do you remember

Bianchetta?" Of course I remembered her. "She's got married," they said. "She's getting on fine."

Nearly every evening Nuto came to see me at the Albergo dell'Angelo and dug me out of the group where I was standing with the doctor and the local secretary and the sergeant-major of the *carabinieri* and the surveyors, and got me talking. Like two brothers we went along the village street under the trees and listened to the cicalas and enjoyed the breeze from the Belbo—in our time we had never come to the village at that hour of the day for we led a different life.

In the moonlight with the black hills round about us, Nuto asked me one night how I had gone about embarking for America and whether I would do it now if I got another chance and could be twenty again. I told him that it hadn't been America that had done it so much as the rage at not being anybody, the wild desire, more than to go away, to come back one fine day after everyone had given me up as dead of hunger. In the village I'd never be anything but a farm-hand, an old Cirino (he had been dead, too, for a while, he'd broken his back falling off a haystack and had lived on for more than a year) so I might as well have a shot at it, and get rid of my urge to cross the sea, now that I'd crossed the Bormida.

"But it isn't easy to get on board ship," said Nuto. "You had courage."

It hadn't been courage, I said to him. I ran away. I might as well tell him about it.

"Do you remember these talks we had with your father in the shop? Even in those days he said people who don't know any better will always be in the dark because the power lies in the hands of men who take good care that ordinary folk don't understand, in the hands, that is, of the government, of the clerical party, of the capitalists. Here at La Mora, it was nothing, but when I had done my military service and wandered through the vennels and the docks at Genoa, I realised what owners and capitalists and the army were. At that time we had the fascists and you couldn't say that sort of thing. But there were the others as well."

I had never told him about it so that we wouldn't get on to the subject—it was pointless, anyway, and now that twenty years had gone past and so much had happened, I didn't even know myself what to believe—but that winter in Genoa I had believed in it and we'd spent so many nights in the conservatory at the villa arguing with Guido and Remo and Cerreti and the rest of them. Then Teresa got the wind up and wouldn't let us in any more and so I told her she could keep on being a servant and being taken a loan of, it served her right, but we wanted to make a stand and fight back. And so we had gone on working in the barracks and the pubs and, after we were discharged, in the shipyards where we found work and in the technical schools we attended in the evenings. Teresa listened to me patiently now and said that I was quite right to study and try to get on and she gave me something to eat in the kitchen. She didn't go back to the subject again, but one night Cerreti came to warn me that Guido and Remo had been arrested and they were looking for the others. Then Teresa, without a word of reproach, spoke to someone—her brother-in-law, her former boss, I don't know which—and in two days she had found me a job as a deck-hand on a boat leaving for America. "That was how it was," I said to Nuto.

"You see how it is," he said. "Sometimes one word is enough to open your eyes, one word heard when you are a boy, spoken by an old man, by a poor old man, like my father. I'm glad you didn't only think of making money. And these friends of yours, how did they die?"

We walked like this along the main road beyond the village and discussed our lot in life. I listened in the moonlight and far off I heard the brake of a cart creaking —a sound that hasn't been heard for a bit on the roads of America. And I thought of Genoa, and the offices, and what my life would have been if they had found me too that morning in the shipyard where Remo worked. In a few days I was going back to the Viale Corsica. Everything was over for the summer.

Someone was running along the road in the dust, it looked like a dog. I saw it was a boy; he was lame and ran towards us. He was on us before. I realised it was Cinto; he flung himself at my legs and howled like a dog.

"What's the matter?"

At first we didn't believe him. He said his father had set fire to the house.

"I bet he has!" said Nuto.

"He has set fire to the house," repeated Cinto. "He tried to kill me. He has hanged himself . . . he has burnt down the house."

"They'll have upset the lamp," I said.

"No, no," he cried. "He has killed Rosina and my grandmother. He wanted to kill me but I didn't let him. Then he set fire to the straw and kept on looking for me, but I had my knife and then he hanged himself in the vineyard. . . ."

Cinto panted and whimpered; he was all black and covered with scratches. He had sat down in the dust on top of my feet and clung to my leg and said again, "My father has hanged himself in the vineyard and burnt the house, and the ox, too. The rabbits ran away but I had my knife. . . . Everything's burnt, the farmer from Piola saw it, too."

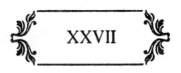

XXVII

NUTO TOOK him by the shoulders and lifted him up the way you lift a young goat.

"Has he killed Rosina and your grandmother?"

Cinto trembled and couldn't answer.

"Has he killed them?" and Nuto shook him.

"Let him alone," I said to Nuto. "He's half-dead. Why don't we go and see?"

Then Cinto clutched my legs and wouldn't hear of it.

"Stand up," I said. "Who were you looking for?"

He was coming to find me and he didn't want to go back to the vineyard again. He had run to call the farmer from Il Morone and the people at Piola; he had wakened them all, and others were running from the hill already and he had shouted to them to put out the fire, but he wouldn't go back to the orchard—he had lost his knife.

"We won't go into the vineyard," I said to him. "We'll stop on the road and Nuto will go up. What are you frightened of? If it's true they came running from the farms, it'll all be out by this time."

We set off, holding him by the hand. We couldn't see the hill at Gaminella from the road with the trees, it was hidden by a spur. But as soon as you left the main road and came round onto the slope which overhangs the Belbo, you'd be bound to see a fire through the trees. We didn't see anything except the misty light of the moon.

Without saying a word, Nuto jerked Cinto's arm and the boy stumbled. We went on, almost running. When we got below the reed-bed, it was evident that something *had* happened. From up there we heard the sound of blows and people shouting to each other as if they were felling a tree, and in the cool night air a cloud of stinking smoke came down over the road.

Cinto didn't offer any resistance, but came on, quickening his pace to match ours, and squeezing my fingers more tightly. People came and went up there at the fig tree, talking all the time. From where I stood on the path I saw in the moonlight the empty space where the hayloft and the stable had been and the gaping walls of the cottage. A red gleam was dying at the foot of the walls, which gave off a black smoke. There was a stink of burnt wool and flesh and dung which caught at the throat. A rabbit made off under my feet.

Nuto halted at the level of the threshing-floor and made a grimace, raising his clenched hands to his forehead.

"That smell," he muttered. "That smell."

The fire was out now, for all the neighbours had run to lend a hand. There had been a moment, they said, when the blaze lit up the watercourse, and you saw the reflection of it in the waters of the Belbo. Nothing had been saved, not even the manure heap at the back.

Someone ran to get the sergeant of the *carabinieri*; they sent a woman to bring something to drink from Il Morone, and they made Cinto swallow a little wine. He asked where the dog was, if it had got burnt, too. Each told his own version of what had happened; we sat Cinto down in the meadow and he told his story in gulps.

How it had begun he didn't know, he had gone down to the Belbo. Then he heard the dog barking and his father tying up the ox. The Signora from the Villa had come with her son to get her share of the beans and potatoes. The Signora had said that two rows of potatoes had been dug already, and so they would have to be made good, and Rosina had cried out at that and Valino had cursed, and the Signora had gone into the house to get the grandmother to speak, while her son kept an eye on the baskets. Then they had weighed the potatoes and the beans and come to an agreement, giving each other dirty looks the while. They had loaded the stuff on to the cart and Valino had gone to the village.

But in the evening, when he came back, he was in a black mood. He had begun to shout at Rosina and the grandmother because they hadn't gathered the beans before. He said that now the Signora was eating the beans that should have been theirs. The old woman was weeping on her mattress.

Cinto himself stood at the door, ready to make off. Then Valino had taken off his belt and begun to beat Rosina. You would have thought he was threshing grain. Rosina had flung herself against the table and was screaming, keeping her hands on her neck. Then she had uttered a more piercing cry, the bottle had fallen, and Rosina, tearing her hair, had thrown herself on top of the grandmother and flung her arms round her. Then Valino had started to kick her—you could hear the sound of the blows—to kick her in the ribs, and he had pounded her with his heavy boots, and Rosina had fallen to the ground and Valino had gone on kicking her in the face and in the stomach.

Rosina was dead, said Cinto, she was dead and blood was pouring from her mouth. "Get up, you fool," said his father. But Rosina was dead, and the old woman was quiet now, too.

Then Valino had started looking for him and he had made off. From the vineyard you couldn't hear anything now, except the dog who tugged at its wire and ran backwards and forwards.

After a while, Valino had begun to call Cinto. Cinto said you could tell from his voice that it wasn't to beat him, but that he was only calling him. He had opened his knife then and made his way to the farmyard. His father was waiting for him on the doorstep, in a black rage. When he saw him with the knife, he said, "You bastard," and tried to catch him. Cinto had made off again.

Then he had heard his father kicking at everything, he had heard him cursing and reviling the priest. Then he had seen the flames.

His father had come outside with the lamp in his hand; the glass was off. He had run all round the house and set fire to the hayloft, too, and the straw, and dashed the lamp against the window. The room where the struggle had been was full of smoke by now. The women didn't come out; he seemed to hear them crying and sobbing.

The whole cottage was ablaze now and Cinto couldn't get down into the field because his father would have seen him as clearly as if it were day. The dog went mad and barked and tore at its wire. The rabbits bolted. The ox was burning, too, in the byre.

Valino had run into the vineyard to look for him with a rope in his hand. Cinto, still clutching the knife, had made off up the watercourse. There he had stayed hidden and seen the glow of the fire above him, reflected against the leaves.

Even from there he could hear the roar of the flames, like a furnace. The dog kept on howling. In the water-course it was as bright as day. When Cinto didn't hear the dog any more or any other sound, he seemed to wake up suddenly and didn't remember what he was doing in the watercourse. Then very quietly he had climbed up towards the walnut tree, clutching the open knife, and on the alert for any sound or sight of the fire. And under the vaulted branches of the walnut tree he had seen his father's feet hanging in the glow from the flames, and the ladder lying on the ground.

He had to repeat this story to the sergeant of the

carabinieri and they showed him his dead father stretched out under a sack, to see if he recognised him. In the meadow they made a heap of the things they had found— the scythe, a wheelbarrow, the ladder, the ox's muzzle and a saddle. Cinto was looking for his knife; he kept asking everyone, and coughing among the stench of smoke and burnt flesh. They told him he would find it all right and that they would be able to get the blades of the hoes and the spades, too, when the embers had cooled. We took Cinto across to Il Morone; it was almost morning and the others had to search the ashes for the remains of the two women.

No one was asleep at Il Morone. The door was open and the fire lit in the kitchen, and the women offered us something to drink; the men sat down to breakfast. It was cool, almost cold. I was sick of arguments and talking. Everyone kept saying the same things. I stayed beside Nuto and walked about the farmyard under the last stars and from up here we saw, in the cold air which had almost a violet tint, the clumps of aspens in the plain and the gleam of water. I had forgotten that the dawn was like that.

Nuto was walking about, hunched up, his eyes on the ground. I said to him at once that we must take charge of Cinto, which was more or less what we'd been doing. He looked at me, his eyes swollen—he seemed half-asleep.

What happened next day was enough to make your blood boil. I heard in the village that the Signora was furious about her property and, seeing that Cinto was the only member of his family living, she claimed that he should pay her compensation or they would put him inside.

It was common knowledge that she had gone to get her lawyer's advice and that he had had to argue with her for an hour. Then she had gone to the priest, too.

The priest made a better job of it. Since Valino had died in mortal sin, he wouldn't hear of pronouncing the benediction over him in the church. They left his coffin outside on the steps while within the priest mumbled over the few blackened bones of the women tied up in a sack. Everything was done secretly, towards evening. The old women from Il Morone, with veils on their heads, went with the dead to the cemetery, gathering daisies and clover by the roadside. The priest didn't go, because when you thought of it, Rosina, too, had lived in mortal sin. But only the dressmaker, who was an old woman with a spiteful tongue, said that.

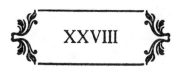

XXVIII

IRENE didn't die of typhus that winter. I remember when I was in the stable or walked along in the rain behind the plough, I tried not to swear any more as long as Irene was in danger, but to think good thoughts instead to help her—for that was what Serafina told us to do. But I don't know if we helped her, perhaps it would have been better if she had died on the day the priest came to give her the benediction. For when she came out of doors at last, in January, and they took her, as thin as a rake, in the gig to hear mass at Canelli, her Cesarino had left for Genoa a while back without having once asked for her himself or got anyone else to ask. And Il Nido was shut up.

When Silvia came back, she had a big disappointment, too, but for all they said, she felt it less. For Silvia was used to these tricks of fate by now and knew how to take them and how to recover from them.

Her Matteo had taken up with someone else. In January Silvia still hadn't come back from Alba, and even at La Mora we began to say that if she didn't come back there was a reason for it—she was pregnant, of course. The ones who went to the market in Alba said that some days Matteo from Crevalcuore went through the square like the shot from a gun, or passed in front of the café. Not that they'd ever been seen going off arm-in-arm or even meeting. So Silvia couldn't go out, so she was pregnant. The truth is that when she returned in the fine weather, Matteo had already taken up with another woman whose father owned the café at Santo Stefano and he spent his nights there. Silvia came back along the main road, holding Santina by the hand; no one had gone to meet them off the train and they stopped in the garden to touch the first roses. They chattered away together as if they were mother and child, red-cheeked after their walk.

It was Irene now who was deadly pale and thin and kept her eyes fixed on the ground. She seemed like the autumn crocuses which come in the meadows after the grape harvest or the grass which keeps on living under a stone. She wore a red handkerchief on her hair, which left her neck and ears uncovered. Emilia said she could never have the head she used to have—Santina would be the golden-haired one now, for her hair was even more beautiful than Irene's. And Santina knew already that she made an impression when she stood behind the gate to let herself be seen, or came amongst us in the farmyard, or along the paths, and chattered away to the women. I asked her what they had done in Alba and what Silvia had done, and if she felt like it she answered that they lived in a fine house with carpets, opposite the church, and some days ladies came with little boys and girls and they played together and ate sweet cakes, and then one evening they had gone to the theatre with their aunt and Nicoletto, and everybody was dressed in their best, and the little girls went to a school kept by the nuns and in another year she would go, too. I didn't manage to learn much of how Silvia spent her time, but she must have danced a lot with the officers. She hadn't ever been ill.

The young men and the girls they had been friendly with began to come to La Mora again. That year Nuto went to do his military service and I was a man now and the grieve no longer took his belt to me and nobody called me bastard. They knew me in many of the farms round about; I came and went in the evening and through the night for I was courting Bianchetta. I was beginning to understand all kinds of things—the scent of the lime-blossom and the acacias had a meaning for me, too, now that I knew what a woman was, knew why the music at the dances made me want to roam about the country-side like a randy dog. The window giving on to the hills beyond Canelli where the fine weather came from and the storms and where the dawn broke, was always the place where the trains steamed away and the road ran past to Genoa. I knew that in two years I would take that train myself, like Nuto. At the festas, I used to go about with the boys of my age group—we drank and sang together and talked about ourselves.

Silvia had lost her head again. Once more Arturo and his friend from Tuscany put in an appearance at La Mora, but she didn't even look at them. She had taken up with an accountant from Canelli who worked on contract and it seemed she must get married this time, for even Sor Matteo appeared to be agreeable—the accountant would come to La Mora on his bicycle, he was a fair-haired boy from San Marzano, and always brought almond cake to Santina—but one evening Silvia disappeared. She didn't come back till the next day, with an armful of flowers. This is what had happened—at Canelli there wasn't only the accountant, but also a fine fellow who knew French and English and came from Milan, tall and grey-haired, a real gentleman—they said he was buying land hereabouts. Silvia would meet him in a villa belonging to friends of theirs and they would lunch together. This time it had been supper and it was next morning when she left the house. The accountant got to know of it and wanted to kill someone, but this Lugli went to see him and talked to him as if he were a boy and the affair ended there.

This man, who was perhaps fifty and had grown-up children, I never saw except in the distance, but for Silvia he was worse than Matteo from Crevalcuore. Matteo and Arturo and all the others were people whom I understood, young men grown up round about, not up to much, certainly, but from our own district, who drank and laughed and spoke like ourselves. But no one knew what this chap from Milan, this Lugli, was doing at Canelli. He gave supper parties at the Croce Bianca, he was on good terms with the mayor and with the local fascists, and visited their factories. He must have promised Silvia to take her to Milan, or some other place, far from La Mora and the hills. Silvia had lost her head and would wait for him at the Café dello Sport and would go about in the car belonging to the party secretary, driving round the country houses and the castles as far as Acqui. I think Lugli was for her what she and her sister could have been for me—what Genoa and Americà were for me later. I knew enough by this time to picture them together and imagine what they would say to each other, how he would tell her about Milan and the theatres and the people with money and the races, and how she would listen eagerly, pretending to know about everything. This Lugli was always dressed like a tailor's dummy, with a pipe in his mouth and a gold ring and gold-filled teeth. Silvia said to Irene once—and Emilia heard her—that he had been in England and was going back there.

But the day came when Sor Matteo lost his temper completely with his wife and daughters. He shouted that he was tired of long faces and late hours, tired of fortune-hunters around the place, tired of never knowing in the evening who was going to do them a bit of good through the night, tired of meeting friends who poked fun at him. He laid the blame on their stepmother and people with too little to do and said all women were whores. He said he'd bring up Santa by himself anyway, and they could marry if anyone would have them, as long as they got out of his road and went back to Alba. Poor man, he was old and couldn't control himself or give orders any more. Lanzone had noticed it, too, when he presented the accounts. We had all noticed it. The end of it was that Irene went red-eyed to bed and Signora Elvira put her arms round Santina and told her not to listen to that sort of thing. Silvia shrugged her shoulders and stayed away all that night and the day after.

So the Lugli episode came to an end, too. It got about that he had made off, leaving huge debts behind him. But this time Silvia turned on him like a cat. She went to the party headquarters at Canelli; she went to the local secretary, she went to the villas where they had had a good time and slept together, and in the end she managed to discover that he must be at Genoa. Then she caught the train to Genoa taking with her what gold she had and the little money she could find.

A month later Sor Matteo went to Genoa to bring her back, after the police had told him where she was because Silvia was of age now and she couldn't be sent home. She was starving on the station platform at Brignole. She hadn't found Lugli or anyone else, and wanted to fling herself under the train. Sor Matteo calmed her and said that it had been an illness, a misfortune, like her sister's attack of typhus, and that they were all expecting her at La Mora. They went home, but this time Silvia was really pregnant.

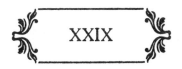

XXIX

ROUND about the same time another piece of news reached us—the old lady at Il Nido had died. Irene didn't say anything, but you could see she was in a fever of excitement, and the colour came back to her cheeks. Now that Cesarino could please himself, they would soon see what kind of a man he was. Rumours flew thick and fast—that he was the sole heir, that the property was divided up, that the old woman had left everything to the bishop and the convents.

Instead, a lawyer came to inspect Il Nido and the lands belonging to it. He didn't speak to anyone, not even to Tomasino. He gave out instructions about the work and the harvest and the sowing. In the house itself he took an inventory. Nuto, who was on leave at that time for the harvest, got to know everything at Canelli. The old lady had left all her possessions to the children of a niece who weren't even counts, and had appointed her lawyer as guardian. So Il Nido remained shut up and Cesarino didn't come back.

At that time I was always around with Nuto and we would speak about all sorts of things, about Genoa and soldiers and music and Bianchetta. He smoked and got me to smoke, too, and asked me if I wasn't fed up yet with walking behind the plough and said it was a big world and there was room for everyone. When he heard the tale about Silvia and Irene, he shrugged his shoulders and said nothing.

Irene didn't say anything either about the news from Il Nido. She was thin still, and deadly pale, and would go and sit with Santina on the banks of the Belbo. She would keep the book on her knee and gaze at the trees. On Sundays she went to mass with a black veil on her head—her stepmother and Silvia, they all went together. One Sunday, it hadn't happened for a long time, I heard her playing the piano again.

The winter before, Emilia had given me a loan of Irene's novels which a girl from Canelli leant to them. For a while back I'd felt like following Nuto's advice and studying something. I wasn't a boy any more to content myself with hearing them speak about the stars and saints' days sitting on the beam after supper. And I read these novels beside the fire to learn something. They told of girls who had guardians and aunts and enemies who kept them shut up in beautiful houses with gardens where there were maids who carried letters and administered poison and stole wills. Then a handsome man would arrive, who kissed them, a man on horseback he was, and at night the girl would feel she was suffocating and go out into the garden, and they would carry her off, and she would awake the next morning in a woodcutter's hut where the handsome man would come to rescue her. Or else the story would start with a boy running wild in the woods, and he was the natural son of the owner of a castle where all sorts of crimes and poisonings took place, and the boy was accused and put in prison, but then a white-haired priest would save him and marry him to the heiress of another castle. I realised I had known these stories for a long time, for Virgilia had told them to Giulia and me in Gaminella—they were the story of the Sleeping Beauty with the golden hair, who was sound asleep in a wood and a hunter awoke her with a kiss; and the story of the wizard with the seven heads who, whenever he had won a maiden's love, became a handsome young man, the son of a king.

I liked these novels, but could Irene and Silvia, who were ladies and had never known Virgilia or cleaned out the stable, really like them too? I realised that Nuto was quite right when he said that to live in a hovel or in a palace was one and the same thing, that blood is the same colour everywhere, and that everybody wants to be rich and in love and make their fortune. On these evenings, coming back beneath the acacias from Bianchetta's house, I was happy; I whistled to myself and thought no more of jumping on to the train.

Signora Elvira had begun to invite Arturo to supper again, but this time he was fly and left his friend from Tuscany at home. Sor Matteo raised no objections. That was before Silvia had told them the state she had come back from Genoa in, and life at La Mora seemed to go on in its accustomed way again, though rather jerkily. Arturo began at once to pay court to Irene, and it was Silvia now, with her hair about her face who would look at him as if she was laughing at him, but when Irene began to play the piano she was off like a shot and leant on the terrace or went for a walk through the fields. She didn't take her parasol any more, for now the women went about with bare heads, even in the heat of the sun.

Irene didn't want to have anything to do with Arturo. She was docile towards him but cold, and she walked with him in the garden and as far as the gate but they hardly ever spoke to each other. Arturo was always the same—he'd used up some more of his father's money and would even wink to Emilia, but we knew that, apart from playing cards and shooting, he wasn't worth much.

It was Emilia who told us that Silvia was pregnant. Emilia got to know it before Silvia's father or any of the rest of them. The evening that Sor Matteo heard the news —Irene and Signora Elvira told him—he started to laugh evilly instead of shouting, and lifted his hand to his mouth. "And now," he sneered through his fingers, "let's get a father for it." But when he made to get up and go into Silvia's room, his head reeled and he fell to the ground. From that day he remained half-paralysed, with his mouth awry.

When Sor Matteo left his bed and was able to take a few steps, Silvia had already seen to things. She had gone to a midwife at Castiglione and had had a clean sweep made. She didn't say anything to anyone. We found out two days later where she had been because the train ticket was still in her pocket. She came back with circles round her eyes and the face of a dead woman— she went to bed and filled it with blood. She died without saying a word to the priest or the others, but she called for her father in a low voice like a little girl.

For the funeral we picked all the flowers in the garden and in the gardens of the farms round about. It was June and there were a lot of flowers. They buried her without her father knowing of it, but he heard the chanting in the next room, and got frightened and tried to say he wasn't dead yet. When later on he came out onto the terrace supported by Signora Elvira and Arturo's father, he had a cap over his eyes and he stayed in the sun without speaking. Arturo and his father took turn about and were always at his side.

The one who didn't take a good view of Arturo any more was Santina's mother. Since the old man was ill it didn't suit her now that Irene should marry and take away her dowry. It was better for her to stay at home unmarried and act as nursemaid to Santina, and so, one day, the little girl would have everything.

Sor Matteo didn't say anything any more—it was all he could do to put a spoon to his mouth. The Signora settled with the grieve and with us, too, and poked her nose in everywhere.

But Arturo was in great form and got his own way. He was doing her a favour if he married Irene now, because after what had happened to Silvia, people were saying that the girls at La Mora were a couple of whores. He didn't say that, but he always came looking terribly serious and kept the old man company and went the errands to Canelli on our horse and gave Irene the holy water in church on Sundays. He was always about, dressed in black; he didn't wear his riding-boots any more and saw to the medicines. Even before he got married he was about the house from morning till night or walking round the farm.

Irene took him so as to get away, so that she wouldn't

see Il Nido on the hill any more or hear her stepmother grumble and rage. She married him in September the year after Silvia died and they didn't make a great splash because of the mourning and because Sor Matteo hardly ever spoke now. They went off to Turin and Signora Elvira complained bitterly to Serafina and Emilia—she'd never have believed that a girl she'd treated as a daughter would have been so ungrateful. At the wedding, Santina was the beauty, all dressed in silk—she was only six, but she looked as if she were the bride.

I went to do my military service that spring and the goings-on at La Mora didn't concern me much any longer. Arturo came back and began to give orders. He sold the piano, he sold the horse, and some of the grazing rights. Irene, who had thought she was going away to live in another house, began to look after her father again and put on his poultices. Arturo was always out of the house now; he took up his card-playing again and his hunting and entertaining friends to supper. By the next year, the only time I came on leave from Genoa, the dowry, half of La Mora, was already spent, and Irene lived at Nizza in a single room and Arturo beat her.

XXX

I REMEMBER a Sunday in summer when Silvia was still alive and Irene was young. I must have been seventeen or eighteen and I was beginning to go the rounds of the villages. It was the first of September, the day of the festa at Buon Consiglio. What with all their tea-parties and visiting and suitors, Silvia and Irene couldn't go—I don't know what was the matter—either it had something to do with their clothes or else they were in a bad temper—in any case they hadn't wanted their usual company, and now they were lolling about on deck-chairs, looking at the sky above the dove-cote. I'd given my neck a good wash that morning and changed my shirt and my boots, and was coming back from the village to have a bite of food and then jump on my bicycle. Nuto had been at Buon Consiglio since the day before, because he was playing for the dancing.

Silvia called to me from the terrace to ask where I was going. She seemed to want to talk. Now and again she spoke to me like this and smiled to me, like the good-looking girl she was, and then I didn't feel I was a servant any longer. But that day I was in a hurry and I was on tenterhooks. Why didn't I take the gig? asked Silvia. I would get there sooner. Then she called to Irene,

"Are *you* not coming to Buon Consiglio, too? Anguilla will take us and look after the horse."

I wasn't very pleased, but I had to stand and wait. They came downstairs with the lunch-basket and parasols and rugs. Silvia had on a flowered dress and Irene wore white. They climbed up in their high-heeled shoes and opened their parasols.

I had given my neck and back a good wash and Silvia stayed near me under the parasol and smelt of flowers. I saw her little pink ear, pierced by the ear-ring, the white nape of her neck and, behind her, Irene's golden head. They were speaking away among themselves about the young men who came to visit them, criticising them and laughing, and they would look at me sometimes and tell me not to listen; then they would start guessing who would be at Buon Consiglio. When we started to climb the hill, I jumped down, not to tire the horse, and Silvia held the reins.

As we went along, they would ask me whose house this was, or whose farm, or what tower that was, and I could judge what the grapes were like, hanging there on the vines, but I didn't know the people who owned them. We turned round to look at the bell-tower at Calosso and I showed them where La Mora lay now.

Then Irene asked me if I really didn't know anything about my own people. I answered that I managed to live quite happily all the same, and it was at that moment that Silvia looked me over from top to toe and said quite seriously to Irene that I was a good-looking boy and didn't even look as if I came from these parts. Irene, not to offend me, said I must have nice hands and I hid them at once. Then she laughed like Silvia, too.

Then they began again to talk about their quarrels and their clothes and we came to Buon Consiglio, under the trees.

There was a confused mass of stalls piled with almond cake and little flags, and there were carts and shooting-booths and you heard from time to time the crack of air-guns. I led the horse into the shade of the plane trees where there were poles to hitch them to, and I un-harnessed the gig and shook out the hay. Irene and Silvia kept asking, "Where are the races, where are the races?" but there was time yet, so they began to look for their friends. I had to keep an eye on the horse and see the fair as well. It was early and Nuto wasn't playing yet, but the air was full of the noise of the instruments, trumpet-ing and squeaking and snorting, each one enjoying a private joke. I found Nuto drinking lemonade with the boys from Seraudi. They were standing in the open space behind the church from where you could see all the hill opposite and the watercourses, as far as the distant farms among the woods. The people who were at Buon Con-siglio came from up there, from the most remote stead-ings and from further away still, from the village beyond the Mango with the little churches, where the only tracks were for goats and no one ever passed by. They had come to the fair in carts and flies, on bicycles and on foot. The place was full of girls, and old women going into the church, and men who were looking round about them. Even the better-off ones, well-dressed girls and little boys wearing ties, were waiting at the door of the church for the service to begin. I told Nuto I had come with Irene and Silvia and we saw them laughing among a crowd of their young men. There were no two ways about it, that flowered dress was the prettiest one there.

We went with Nuto to see the horses in the stables at the inn. Bizzarro from the Station stopped us at the door and told us to keep watch. He and the others uncorked a bottle and half of it spilled on the ground. But they'd no intention of drinking it. They poured out the wine still foaming, into a bowl, and made Laiolo, who was as black as pitch, lick it up, and when he had drunk it all, they gave him four cuts with the handle of a whip on his hind-legs, to waken him up. Laiolo began to let fly with his feet, arching his back like a cat. "Not a word about this," they said. "You'll see, we'll win the flag."

At that very moment, Silvia and her young men appeared on the threshold.

"If you've taken to drinking already," said a fat youth who was always laughing, "*you*'ll be running instead of the horses."

Bizzarro began to laugh and mopped his face with a red handkerchief.

"It's these young ladies who should do the running," he said, "they're lighter on their feet than us."

Then Nuto went off to play for the procession with the Madonna. They lined up in front of the church and then the Madonna came out. Nuto winked to us and spat, wiped his mouth with his hand and put the clarinet to his lips. They played a tune you could have heard down at the Mango.

I liked being in this open space among the plane trees,

hearing the sound of the trumpets and the clarinet and seeing all the people kneeling down and running about and the Madonna coming out of the big door, swaying on the shoulders of the sacristans. Then came the priests, the boys in their surplices, the old women, the gentry, the incense, and all the candles in the sunshine, the brightly coloured dresses, and the young girls. And the men and women from the stalls, from the cake stall and the shooting-booth and the merry-go-round, were all standing watching, under the plane trees.

The Madonna was carried round the square and some-one set off crackers. I saw Irene with her golden hair, putting her fingers in her ears. I was happy because it was I who'd brought them in the gig and because I was at the festa with them.

I went over for a moment to draw the hay together again where the horse could reach it and I stopped to have a look at our rug and shawls and lunch-basket.

Then came the race and the music began again while the horses were coming out on to the road. But I had one eye always open for the flowered dress and the white one; I saw that they were talking and laughing and I'd have given anything to be one of these young men and partner them in the dancing.

The race passed us twice, once downhill and once up, under the plane trees, and the horses made a noise like the Belbo in flood; Laiolo was carrying a young man we didn't know; he rode hunched up and was using his whip like a madman. I was standing beside Bizzarro, who began to swear, then he shouted Hurrah, when another horse lost its footing and came down on its nose and lay like a sack; then he swore again when Laiolo raised its head and jumped; he tore the handkerchief from his neck and said, "You bastard!" and the boys from Seraudi were dancing about and butting each other like goats; then the people began to shout somewhere else, and Bizzarro turned a somersault, big as he was, and hit his head on the ground; everybody was still shouting; a horse from Neive had won.

Afterwards I lost sight of Irene and Silvia. I made the rounds of the shooting-booths and the card-tables and I went to the inn to listen to the horses' owners who were quarrelling and drinking one bottle of wine after another and the parish priest was trying to make peace amongst them. Some were singing and some were cursing and some were eating salami and cheese. No girls were going to come into this courtyard, that was one sure thing.

By this time Nuto and the band were sitting on the dancing floor and getting down to it. You could hear them playing and laughing in the still air; the evening was cool and clear and I wandered about behind the booths and saw the sackcloth partitions billowing up, and the young men were joking and drinking and some of them had already begun to lift the skirts of the women at the stalls. The boys were shouting and pinching almond cake from each other and making a din.

I went to watch the dancing on the platform in the big marquee. The boys from Seraudi were dancing already. Their sisters were there, too, but I stayed to watch because I was looking for the flowered dress and the white one. I saw them both in the light of the acetylene lamp, in the arms of their young men, their faces on their shoulders as the sound of the music bore them along. "I wish I was Nuto," I thought. I went along beside Nuto's seat and made him fill my glass, too, as if I were one of the band.

Then Silvia found me lying in the meadow, beside the horse's head. I was lying stretched out counting the stars through the leaves of the plane trees when, all of a sudden, I saw her happy face and her flowered dress between me and the vault of the sky. "He's here sleeping," she shouted.

Then I jumped up and their young men got noisy and wanted them to stay longer. In the distance, behind the church, girls were singing. One of the young men offered to walk home with them. But there were the other young ladies who said, "And what about us?"

We set off by the light of the acetylene lamp, then I went slowly downhill along the dark road, listening to the sound of the hooves. The choir behind the church were still singing. Irene had wrapped herself up in a shawl. Silvia went on and on talking about the people and her partners and the summer, and she criticised them all and laughed. She asked if I had a girl of my own. I said I had been with Nuto watching him play.

Then gradually Silvia calmed down and the wonderful moment came when she laid her head on my shoulder, and smiled at me and said could she keep it there while I drove. I held the reins and kept my eyes on the horse's ears.

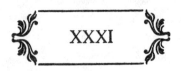

XXXI

Nuto took Cinto into his house to make him learn carpentry and teach him to play the clarinet. We agreed that, if the boy turned out well, I would get him a job in Genoa in due course. Another thing we had to decide was whether to take him to the hospital at Alessandria to let the doctor see his leg. Nuto's wife protested that the house at Salto was too full already, between apprentices and joiner's benches, and she couldn't keep an eye on him properly. We told her that Cinto was a good child. But I took him aside again and explained that he must be careful, here it wasn't like the road at Gaminella—cars, trucks and motor-cycles, coming and going to Canelli, passed in front of the shop, and he must always look before he crossed.

And so Cinto found a place to live in and I had to leave the next day for Genoa. I spent the forenoon at Salto and Nuto was always at my heels. "So you're going away," he said. "Aren't you coming back for the grape harvest?"

"But I'm maybe going on a ship," I said. "I'll come back for the festa another year."

Nuto pursed his lips, as he always does. "You haven't been here very long," he said to me. "We haven't really spoken to each other."

I laughed.

"I've found you another son, anyway."

When we rose from the table, Nuto made up his mind. He snatched up his jacket as he went past and looked up.

"Let's go over to the other side," he muttered, "that's your part of the world."

We crossed the plantation and the footbridge over the Belbo and came out on to the road at Gaminella, among the acacias.

"Let's have a look at the house," I said. "Valino was a human being, too."

We climbed up the path. It was a skeleton with black, gaping walls, and now above the rows of vines we could see the walnut tree which looked enormous.

"Only the trees are left," I said. "It was a good job Valino took the bill-hook to them. . . . The watercourse has had the best of it."

Nuto stood silent and looked round the courtyard, full of stones and cinders. I wandered about among the stones and I couldn't even find the mouth of the cellar, the ruins had blocked it. In the watercourse birds were making a din and some of them were fluttering, unchecked, about the vines.

"I'm going to eat a fig," I said. "There's no harm in it now."

I took the fig and remembered the taste.

"The Signora at the villa," I said, "I wouldn't put it past her to make me spit it out."

Nuto said nothing and looked at the hill.

"And now they are dead, too," he said. "What a lot of people have died since you left La Mora."

Then I sat down on the beam which was still the same and told him that even all these deaths couldn't put Sor Matteo's daughters out of my head. "Let's leave out Silvia, she died at home. But Irene and that good-for-nothing, living the life she has lived. And Santina, I wonder how Santina died?"

Nuto was playing about with some stones and now he looked up.

"Don't you want to go further up the hill? Come on, it's early."

So we set off and he went in front along the paths through the vineyards. I remembered the pale, dry earth, the smooth slippery grass of the paths, and the smell of grapes which belongs to the hill and the vineyard, with its promise already of harvesting grapes in the sunshine. In the sky there were long mare's-tails and white flossy clouds which seemed like the bright drift we see at night in the darkness behind the stars. I was thinking that tomorrow I'd be in the Viale Corsica when suddenly I realised that the sea, too, is veined with the lines of the currents and that when, as a child, I watched the clouds and the path of the stars, I had already started on my travels without knowing it.

Nuto waited for me on the bank and said, "You didn't see Santa when she was twenty. It would have been worth it. She was more beautiful than Irene with eyes like the black heart of a poppy. But she was a bitch, a damned bitch. . . ."

I stopped to look down into the valley. As a boy, I'd never climbed as far as this. You could see a long way, as far as the little houses at Canelli and the Station and the dark wood at Calamandrana. I knew that Nuto was going to tell me something, and I remembered Buon Consiglio, I don't know why.

"I went there once with Silvia and Irene," I said for something to say, "in the gig. I was a boy then. From up there you could see even the most distant villages, the farms, the farmyards, even the marks above the windows where the vines have been sprayed. There was the horse-race and we behaved as if we were all mad. . . . I don't even remember now who won. I remember only the farms on the hills and Silvia's dress, pink and mauve, with flowers on it."

"And Santa, too," said Nuto, "once got us to take her to a fair at Bubbio. There was one year she would come to dance only when I was playing. Her mother was still alive . . . they were still staying at La Mora."

He turned round and said, "Are you coming?"

He started to go in front of me again up the slopes. From time to time he would look about him, trying to find a path. I was thinking how everything happens again as it has happened before—I saw Nuto in the gig driving Santa up the braes to the fair, as I had driven her sisters. In the rocks above the vineyards I saw the first of those little caves where they keep the hoes, or, if there is a spring beside it, there in the shade, hanging over the water, grows maidenhair fern. We crossed a vineyard; it wasn't in good heart and was full of bracken and those little yellow flowers with the hard stem which seem to go with mountains—I've always known that you chewed them and put them on a cut to make it close up. And the hill still rose in front of us; we had already passed several farms and now we came out into the open.

"I might as well tell you," said Nuto unexpectedly without raising his eyes; "I know how they killed Santa, I was there myself."

He started to go along the road which was almost level and led round a crest. I didn't say anything but let him do the speaking. I watched the road and barely turned my head each time a bird or a hornet swooped at me.

There was a time, began Nuto, when he looked up to see if the curtains moved every time he was in Canelli and passed along the road behind the cinema. There was plenty of talk about it. Nicoletto was at La Mora and Santa, who couldn't bear him, had run off to Canelli the moment her mother was dead, taken a room, and begun to teach. But being the girl she was, she'd at once found a job in the fascist party rooms, and there was talk of a militia officer, of a *podestà*, of the local fascist secretary, in fact of all the most criminal types in the neighbourhood. Such a well-brought-up girl with such fair hair, it was right and proper for her to jump into the car and drive around the district and have supper in the villas and the big houses and go to the Spa at Acqui, if it hadn't been for the company she kept. Nuto tried not to see her in the streets, but when he passed under her window, he looked up at the curtains.

Then, with the summer of 1943, this good time came to an end for Santa, too. Nuto, who was always about Canelli to pick up news and pass it on, hadn't looked up at her curtains any more. People said that Santa had run off to Alessandria with her militia lieutenant.

Then September came and the Germans returned and the war with them; the soldiers came home to hide, in other people's clothes, barefoot and starving, and the fascists kept on firing all night long and everybody said, "We knew it would end like this." This was the republic. One fine day, Nuto heard that Santa had come back to Canelli and taken on her job again at the party rooms; she was getting drunk and going to bed with the blackshirts.

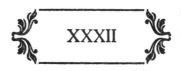

XXXII

HE HADN'T believed it. Up to the very last, he hadn't believed it. He saw her once crossing the bridge, she was coming from the Station and she was wearing a grey fur coat and suede shoes and her eyes were shining with the cold. She had stopped him.

"How are things at Salto? Do you still play? Oh Nuto, I was afraid you were in Germany, too. It must be bad up there. Do they leave you alone?"

To go through Canelli in these days was always dangerous. There were the patrols, the Germans. And a girl like Santa wouldn't have spoken to a boy like Nuto in the street if it hadn't been for the war. He was on edge that day and merely answered yes and no.

Then he had seen her again at the Caffè dello Sport; it was she who had called to him as she came out of the door. Nuto was watching the people going in, but it was a peaceful sunny morning, one of those Sundays when people go to mass.

"You used to see me when I was so high," said Santa, "you believe what I say. They're a bad lot in Canelli, some of them. They'd burn me if they could. They don't want a girl to make anything of her life. They'd like to see me finishing up like Irene and kissing the hand that strikes me—pitiful creatures that haven't even the guts to be blackguards."

Santa was smoking cigarettes which you couldn't get at Canelli and she'd offered some to him.

"Take some," she said; "take the lot. There are so many of you who smoke up there.

"You see how it is," said Santa. "Just because I was friendly with someone once and had my fling, even you turned away and looked in the windows when I passed. Yet you knew my mother, you knew me and what I'm like, you took me to the festa. Do you think I wasn't angry, too, with that set of cowards we used to have?—the ones we have now at least stand up for themselves. Now I've got to live and eat their bread, because I've always worked for myself—no one has ever kept me, but if I were to speak out, I would lose my temper."

Santa was saying this at the marble table, looking at Nuto without a smile on her face, with that delicately formed shameless mouth of hers and her great moist angry eyes, like her sisters'. Nuto tried hard to see if she was lying and eventually told her that these are times when you have to make up your mind to be on one side or the other and that he had made up his mind and was on the same side as the deserters and the partisans and the

184

communists. He should have asked her to act as their spy at the command posts, but he hadn't dared—he couldn't stomach the idea of making a woman, especially Santa, run such risks.

But Santa thought of it and told Nuto a lot about troop movements, about the circulars the command sent out and what the *repubblichini* were saying. Another day she sent word to him not to come to Canelli because it was dangerous, and the Germans did indeed raid the squares and the cafés. Santa said that she herself ran no risks, that they were old acquaintances of hers and worthless ones at that who came to her to get things off their chests and that they'd have sickened her if it hadn't been for the information she was able to pass on to the partisans. The morning that the blackshirts shot the two boys under the plane trees and left them lying like dogs, Santa came on her bicycle to La Mora and from there to Salto and spoke to Nuto's mother, telling her if they had a rifle or a pistol to hide it in the watercourse. Two days later the blackshirts came that way and turned the house upside down.

And there came the day when Santa took Nuto by the arm and told him she couldn't stand it any longer. She couldn't go back to La Mora because Nicoletto was unbearable and the job at Canelli, after all these deaths, was too much for her and driving her out of her mind; if this sort of life didn't end quickly, she'd lay hold on a pistol and shoot someone—she knew whom—herself maybe.

"I'd take to the hills, too," she said, "but I can't. They'd shoot me on sight. I'm the woman from the fascist headquarters."

Then Nuto took her up the watercourse and got her to meet Baracca. She told Baracca what she'd done already. Baracca stood and listened with his eyes on the ground. When she'd finished, he said only, "Go back to Canelli."

"But I can't . . ." said Santa.

"Go back to Canelli and wait for orders from us. We'll send you them."

Two months later—it was the end of May—Santa ran off from Canelli because she had been warned they were coming to arrest her. The owner of the cinema told me that a German patrol had gone in to search the house. It was the talk of Canelli. Santa took to the hills and joined the partisans. Nuto happened to hear about her from someone who was passing through with a message during the night, and they all said she carried arms like the rest of them and had won their respect. If it hadn't been for the sake of his old mother and the fear of the house being burnt over their heads, Nuto would have joined the band, too, to help her.

But Santa didn't need his help. When the mopping-up operations took place in June and so many died along these paths, Santa fought a whole night through with Baracca in a farm building behind Superga and came to the door herself to shout to the fascists that she knew every one of them and they didn't put the wind up her. The next morning she and Baracca made off.

Nuto told me all this in a low voice, stopping every so often to look around him; he gazed at the stubble-fields, at the bare vineyards, at the slope which was beginning to get steep again, and said, "Let's go this way." The point we had reached now couldn't even be seen from the Belbo; everything was small and far away and hidden in the mist; round about us were only distant ridges and high peaks. "Did you know that Gaminella stretched so far?" he asked me.

We stopped at the top of a vineyard, in a hollow sheltered by acacias. We saw the blackened ruin of a house. Nuto said quickly, "The partisans were there. The Germans burnt it down.

"Two boys with guns came to get me at Salto one evening. I knew them. We took the same road as we came today. We walked on although night had already fallen, for they couldn't tell me what Baracca wanted. When we passed by the farms the dogs barked, no one stirred, not a light showed—you know what it was like at that time. I wasn't very happy."

Nuto had seen a light under the door. He saw a motor-cycle in the courtyard, and blankets, and one or two boys, not many—their camp was in the woods, farther down.

Baracca said that he'd sent for him to hear an ugly bit of news—there was proof that this Santa of theirs was acting as a spy, that she had directed the mopping-up operations in June and had brought about the collapse of the committee of national liberation at Nizza, and even captured Germans had had her messages on them, reporting dumps to the fascist headquarters.

Baracca was an accountant from Cuneo, he was all there, he'd been in Africa, too, and he didn't talk much —you know he died with the boys at La Neve. He told Nuto he still didn't understand why Santa had fought beside him that night of the mopping-up operations.

"It would be because you have a way with women," said Nuto, but he was in despair and his voice shook.

Baracca said that Santa had a way with people, too, if she felt like it. And that was what had happened. She'd smelt danger and—this was the last straw—she'd gone off with two of their best men. Their job now was to take her at Canelli. The orders were already in writing.

"Baracca kept me three days up there, partly to relieve his feelings by talking to me about Santa, and partly to make sure I wouldn't get mixed up in it. One morning Santa came back, under escort. She no longer wore the windbreaker and the slacks she had worn all these months. To come out of Canelli she had put on women's clothes again and when the partisans had stopped her up by Gaminella, she'd got a shock. She had on her information about orders the fascists were sending out. But it didn't help her any. In our presence Baracca read out to her the numbers of those who had deserted at her instigation, the number of dumps we had lost, the number of men who had died because of her. Santa sat on a chair and listened, completely disarmed. She stared at me angrily, trying to catch my eye. Then Baracca read out the sentence and told two of them to take her outside. They were more bewildered than she was. They'd always seen her wearing her jacket and belt and they couldn't get used to the idea that now they had a hold of her, she was dressed in white. They took her outside. She turned round at the door and looked at me and made a face just like a child. But, once outside, she tried to run away. We heard a cry and someone running and a burst of tommy-gun fire which seemed endless. We ran out, too, and saw her lying on the grass in front of the acacias."

Even more clearly than Nuto did, I saw Baracca—he had been hanged, too, until he was dead. I looked at the black ruined walls, I looked round me and asked if Santa was buried here.

Mightn't they find her some day? They found the other, too. . . .

Nuto had sat down on the wall and looked at me with his obstinate eyes.

"No, not Santa," he said. "You won't find her. You can't cover a woman like her with earth and leave her like that. There were still too many men who wanted her. Baracca saw to that. He made us cut a lot of twigs in the vineyard and we piled them on top of her until we had enough. Then we poured petrol on the pile and set fire to it. By midday, everything was burnt to ashes. Last year the mark was still there, like the bed of a bonfire."

ALLAN MASSIE

AUGUSTUS

AUGUSTUS reconstructs the lost memoirs of Augustus, true founder of the Roman Empire, son of Julius Caesar, friend and later foe of Mark Antony, patron of Horace and Virgil. Massie has breathed conviction and realism into one of the greatest periods of the past, creating an unforgettable array of characters and incidents.

'All the drama of Graves's *I, Claudius* with an added mordant humour'
Harriet Waugh in the Spectator

'He makes Augustus credible as a man: wily, ruthless, shrewd, generous, admirable'
Andrew Sinclair in The Times

'A private and public history that never loses its pace or grip. Massie summons up a Roman scene that frankly exists as much in the late twentieth century as in the first century B.C.'
Boyd Tonkin in The Listener

'A great achievement by any standard'
The Scotsman

'A marvellous historical novel, written with style and verve . . . ranks with Robert Graves's classics *I, Claudius* and *Claudius The God*. All the colour, cruelty and splendour of a great pagan civilisation are given their due by a novelist at the height of his powers'
Dublin Sunday Press

sceptre

RONALD FRAME

SANDMOUTH PEOPLE

'A major new novel'
Susan Hill

'A genuine piece of original writing . . . dealing with one day (St George's Day) in the life of a small but wealthy English seaside town in the 50s. This is a marvellous picture of England at a fixed point of time. Mr Frame has caught his characters in a sort of literary aspic. Ambitious as any literary effort so far this year and, what's more, a thoroughly good read'
Stanley Reynolds in Punch

'One of our most gifted younger writers'
The Times

'Ambitious . . . he writes stylishly and wittily and takes a great stride forward with this book. It's also cleverly plotted and builds up to an unexpected climax'
Susan Hill in Good Housekeeping

'A triumph'
William Leith in The Guardian

'Inventive and persuasive. The success of the novel lies in the skill with which Mr Frame depicts the gap between appearance and reality, and his sense that we "can't get away from the past" make this a compelling novel, one that feeds the readers' imagination and is likely to linger in the memory when far more self-assertive and less subtle books have faded'
Allan Massie, author of AUGUSTUS and Booker Prize Judge, 1987, in The Scotsman

sceptre

Current and forthcoming titles from Sceptre

ALLAN MASSIE

AUGUSTUS

RONALD FRAME

SANDMOUTH PEOPLE

KERI HULME

THE WINDEATER

MELVYN BRAGG

THE MAID OF BUTTERMERE

URSULA BENTLEY

PRIVATE ACCOUNTS

BOOKS OF DISTINCTION